"Why did you come looking for me, Mitch?" Kelly asked. **"I buried you a long time ago."**

He set the coffee cup on the counter, then suddenly reached across the narrow space. She felt a cool touch against her throat near the neckline of her blouse, but before she could stiffen or pull away, he had slipped one finger beneath the thin gold chain and drawn it toward him. As he pulled the chain taut, the diamond ring lifted from its resting place and hung suspended, glittering in the sunlight.

Kelly stared at the ring, then looked at Mitch. For the first time he was smiling. "I don't think so," he said quietly.

For a long moment she stared at him with huge violet eyes. Then she pulled the ring away from him. "Don't read too much into that," she said stiffly.

"What can I read into it, except the truth? You wouldn't still be wearing that ring if you really had buried me. You still feel something."

She shook her head. "I felt too much for too long. Then one day I just stopped feeling. I'm sorry for what we lost, but I can't bring it back."

"Maybe not. But I have to try, Kelly. I don't have a choice. For me, nine years passed in a night. I woke up loving you."

She felt a pain so sharp she couldn't breathe for a moment. "Not me, Mitch. I'm not her anymore. I became someone else while you were sleeping. The girl you loved is dead, Mitch. Let go of her, and get on with your life."

He was silent, his gaze so intense it was like an actual touch. "I won't lose you too, Kelly. Not without a fight. . . .

WHAT ARE *LOVESWEPT* ROMANCES?

They are stories of true romance and touching emotion. We believe those two very important ingredients are constants in our highly sensual and very believable stories in the *LOVESWEPT* line. Our goal is to give you, the reader, stories of consistently high quality that may sometimes make you laugh, sometimes make you cry, but are always fresh and creative and contain many delightful surprises within their pages.

Most romance fans read an enormous number of books. Those they truly love, they keep. Others may be traded with friends and soon forgotten. We hope that each *LOVESWEPT* romance will be a treasure—a "keeper." We will always try to publish

LOVE STORIES YOU'LL NEVER FORGET
BY AUTHORS YOU'LL ALWAYS REMEMBER

The Editors

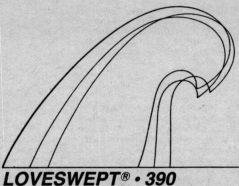

LOVESWEPT® • 390

Kay Hooper
What Dreams May Come

BANTAM BOOKS
NEW YORK • TORONTO • LONDON • SYDNEY • AUCKLAND

Grateful acknowledgment is made for permission
to reprint "And Death Shall Have No Dominion,"
Dylan Thomas: Poems of Dylan Thomas. Copyright 1943
by New Directions Publishing Corporation. Reprinted by
permission of New Directions Publishing Corporation.

WHAT DREAMS MAY COME
A Bantam Book / April 1990

If you would be interested in receiving protective vinyl
covers for your Loveswept books, please write to this address
for information:

Loveswept
Bantam Books
P.O. Box 985
Hicksville, NY 11802

ISBN 0-553-44022-5

Published simultaneously in the United States and Canada

PRINTED IN THE UNITED STATES OF AMERICA

OPM   0 9 8 7 6 5 4 3 2 1

Author's Note

For both Sleeping Beauty and Rip Van Winkle, sleep was an escape. The princess slept to avoid the fatal consequences of a wicked fairy's curse, and Rip slept to avoid a nagging wife—among other things. She woke to find her world little changed, with a handsome prince and the promise of happily ever after; he woke to changes, but after some understandable confusion found his life a happier one.

But, what if sleep weren't an escape? What if a man woke to find that years had been stolen from him, that the world had gone on without him, and that his sole tie to the life that had been his was the woman he loved?

What if . . .

To sleep: perchance to dream:
ay, there's the rub;
For in that sleep of death
what dreams may come . . .
—Shakespeare, *Hamlet*

Some come to take their ease
And sleep an act or two.
—Shakespeare, *Henry VIII*

The moon has set . . . it is midnight,
and time passes, and I sleep alone.
—Sappho

Prologue

February 14, 1980

"I can't accept that."

"You have to. It's been nearly two months; his condition hasn't changed in any way. We've called in every specialist available, and they all agree."

She stared out the window of the hospital waiting room, oblivious to the bleak, gray midwinter scene but feeling as cold as the rain trickling down the panes of glass. Unwilling to look at the familiar compassion in his tired eyes, she didn't turn to face the doctor.

Not again. She had gazed with desperate hope into those eyes day after day for weeks, praying for a different response from him. But day after day the doctor's weary eyes had remained pitying, offering no hope, and, with a tiny shake of his head, he always indicated there was no change.

The tearing pain and dreadful fear had turned into cold numbness, and she was grateful for it. It had been too much to bear, the pain and fear—

and grief. Losing her brother so suddenly, and at the same time facing the possibility of losing Mitch as well. The first week had been the worst because nothing had been able to blunt the shock, and there had been so many things she'd had to take care of, arrangements to be made. Her parents had been devastated, and it had fallen on her to do what had to be done.

She had gotten through the funeral somehow, just as she had packed up Keith's things and put them in storage. She had dropped out of college for a semester, dividing her time between home and the hospital. The weeks had passed with agonizing slowness, and yet it seemed that only yesterday she had been eyeing gaily wrapped packages underneath a Christmas tree and waiting impatiently for Mitch to arrive at her house; Keith had gone to pick him up because Mitch's car had broken down the day before.

They never made it home that night. And now she was here, listening to a compassionate doctor's gentle voice telling her that the date she had made with Mitch on Christmas Eve would in all probability never be kept.

"He's alive," she said huskily without turning, clinging to that slim hope. "He's breathing on his own. And you said—you told me he wasn't brain dead."

The doctor sighed. "His brain is functioning, but we can't be sure there's been no damage. A coma of this duration almost inevitably means damage—"

"Almost," she murmured.

"Miss Russell, I can't be positive about anything. There's still so much we don't know about the brain. And, yes, people have survived comas of extended duration with little or no lasting damage. But those cases are so rare, they're only footnotes in the medical journals. The probability is that John Mitchell will never regain consciousness."

She was silent.

"I've spoken to his father," the doctor said tiredly. "He wants to move his son to a private constant-care facility."

"Why should he make that decision?" Her voice was tight now. "He never gave a damn about Mitch; he hasn't even been here since the accident."

"He has the right to make the decisions for his son because the court granted him legal guardianship; you know that. I understand they were estranged, but he has assumed responsibility for his son's welfare. The facility he's chosen is the best—but it's also five hundred miles away. There's no objection to your continuing to visit Mr. Mitchell."

"How kind," she said bitterly, knowing that visits would be nearly impossible once Mitch was moved so far away. She had to return to college, and to her part-time job; her family had little money.

The doctor drew a breath and made a final attempt. "Miss Russell, if you were my daughter, I'd give you the same advice I'm about to give you now: Get on with your life."

After a long moment she said, "Thank you, Dr. Ryan." Her voice was quiet, toneless.

He left the room, knowing that the attempt had failed. Kelly Russell wasn't prepared to bury John Mitchell.

Feeling very old, she stood at the window, her eighteenth birthday just months behind her. She pressed her fingers lightly against the cold glass and watched the rain trickle down. On the third finger of her slim hand a diamond solitaire caught the faint light and glittered.

They were too young, her parents had said worriedly. Especially she. But they had known Mitch since he and Keith had met in high school, and since he had told them quite firmly on Kelly's fifteenth birthday that he'd marry her as soon as she was old enough, they couldn't say they hadn't had time to get used to the idea. In love with her brother's best friend for as long as she could remember, Kelly had never wavered in her feelings—and neither had Mitch.

He had gone to college, working just as Keith had to put himself through school. Only after he graduated and found a good job had he announced —with Kelly's entire family present—his intention of marrying her. Reassuring her somewhat dazed parents, he had promised they'd wait until after Kelly graduated from high school. He had even been willing to wait while she went to college, but Kelly had protested that she could continue her schooling after they were married.

And so the date had been set. They had, she thought now dully, done everything right. Mitch had a good job with a healthy income and a promising future; he had been living in the apartment they'd chosen together while she continued to live with her family. They had seen each other on weekends and occasional evenings, spending the time planning their life together. They had done everything right. But they hadn't counted on fate.

She stared at the bright diamond on her finger, and for the first time in weeks felt the wetness of tears on her cheeks.

Today should have been her wedding day.

"Mitch," she whispered.

He blinked drowsily at the pattern of morning sunlight on the ceiling. The light was so bright it made his eyes hurt; he thought it must have snowed during the night, because the reflected glare was fierce.

He muttered a curse, and the cracked, hoarse sound of his own voice so startled him that the words broke off abruptly. His voice? That didn't sound like his voice. And there was something wrong with his eyes. No, one eye. Only his right eye seemed to be open. He felt coldness spread slowly inside him, and a nameless uneasiness stirred in his mind like something fearful rustling in the darkness. He wanted to sit up and fling back the covers, but was suddenly conscious of the heavy weight of his own body.

"Oh, my God . . ."

The voice was feminine and unfamiliar. With a tremendous effort he managed to turn his head until he saw her. Through one eye, still only one eye, what was wrong with his left one? She was standing in the open doorway, dressed in the white uniform of a nurse. Her eyes were wide with shock, her pretty face pale, and she was gripping the doorjamb tightly.

"Who're you?" he muttered in that hoarse, rasping, foreign voice. Before she could answer, he realized that he was in a hospital bed, and the nameless fear stirred again in his mind. "Where the hell am I?" he demanded.

"I—I'll be right back, Mr. Mitchell," she whispered, and fled almost, it seemed, in a panic.

He nearly called her back, because he didn't

want to be alone. He tried to sit up, and a cold sweat broke out on his brow when he realized it was impossible; he could feel muscles twitching, but there was no strength in them. Dear Lord, what had happened? Had he been injured somehow? Try as he would, he couldn't remember. With all his will he concentrated on lifting his right hand toward his face. The nurse had looked so shocked; had his face been damaged? Was that why he couldn't see out of his left eye? Did he look like some kind of monster?

He was lying flat on his back, and it was endless moments before he saw his hand wavering unsteadily, as if it weren't connected to the rest of him. He couldn't move his upper arm at all, but managed to move his head a little until his fingers touched his chin. With that accomplished, he was able to shakily explore the right side of his face. No bandages, no injuries that he could feel. Afraid of what he was going to find, he turned his head a bit more so that his fingers could reach the left side.

His teeth clamped together hard as he felt the sutures neatly closing his left eyelid. Fighting the queasiness rising in his throat, he forced himself to probe gently. Gone. His left eye was gone. But at least he was no monster; he couldn't find any other evidence of injury. There was definitely something more wrong, though. The bones of his face were too prominent, as if he'd lost a great deal of weight.

Sweating and panting from the effort, he allowed his hand to fall weakly back to his side. All right, then. He'd lost an eye. What about the rest of him? Why did his body feel so heavy, almost as if it didn't belong to him? Nearly groaning with the strain, he managed to lift his head a few inches so he could see himself. The reassuring presence of his feet under the blankets was obvious, and his left arm was there all right.

Dear God, was he paralyzed too?

He glared at his toes and willed them to move, rewarded finally with a twitch from each foot. He couldn't lift his left arm, but the fingers moved slightly. Exhausted, he let his head fall back as he tried to catch his breath, closing his eye and very conscious of his pounding heart.

He heard quick footsteps and opened his eye again to look up at the man bending over his bed. The white coat identified him as a doctor, and unlike the nurse, his eyes gleamed with excitement rather than panic.

"Do you know your name?" he said slowly and clearly.

"Of course I know my name. I'm John Mitchell." He was so annoyed by the question that his voice came out as little more than a growl. "Where the hell am I? A hospital? What happened?"

"Wait. Let me raise the head of the bed a little." The doctor pressed a button and the bed hummed.

Mitch could feel his body protesting the movement, and bit back a groan. His head swam dizzily, and he had to close his eye for a few moments until the nausea passed. When he was able to look again, the doctor was sitting in a chair by the bed and watching him intently.

"I'm Dr. Brady. Have you tried to move?"

"Yes. And I can. But just barely."

"Good. We were sure there was no spinal damage, but the muscles have weakened."

"Why can I barely move?" Mitch asked hoarsely. "What happened to me?"

"You were in an accident. A car accident, on Christmas Eve. Do you remember?"

Frowning, Mitch searched his mind. "No. I don't remember anything about that."

"Don't worry, it isn't unusual. You may never remember the hours just before the crash."

"How badly was I hurt?"

"A number of broken bones and some internal injuries. But all that has healed. Your left eye is gone, but there isn't much scarring and the socket's intact if you decide to use a glass eye." The doctor's voice was calm and impersonal. "You'll need physical therapy to get your muscles and nerves back in working order, and it'll take time, but you should be as good as new."

Mitch felt the dark stirrings in his mind again, the rustle of panic. He looked down at his body, looked at the arms that were too thin, remembered touching a face with little flesh. Holding his voice as steady as possible, he said, "Broken bones and internal injuries take time to heal. Lots of time. Why can't I remember that, Doc? What else happened to me?"

Softly, the doctor said, "You've been in a coma, Mr. Mitchell."

He understood what that meant, but only vaguely. A coma was like a sleep, a long sleep. His mind told him he had slept only a night, but his body—a new thought entered his mind, replacing the nameless fears with one that was very real.

"Was I alone?" he asked hoarsely. "In the car?"

The doctor frowned, studying him, then said slowly, "I was told a friend of yours was driving. The accident wasn't his fault; a drunk driver crossed the median and crashed into you."

Mitch felt cold. "Keith? How is he?"

"I'm sorry. He didn't make it."

The coldness spread through him. Keith . . . his best friend since the first year of high school, like a brother. Lord, what Kelly must be going through! Pain and grief ached inside him, but even that could no longer hold back the icy certainty that the accident had stolen more than his best friend and his eye.

"How long?" he demanded, bracing himself for a reply he somehow knew would be devastating. "How long have I been in a coma?"

Dr. Brady hesitated. "Mr. Mitchell, I want to remind you that you are extremely lucky to be alive. No one expected you to come out of the coma. With therapy, your physical condition should be optimum within a few months, a year at most. Judging by your coherency, I'd venture to say there's been no brain damage, though you may discover more gaps in your memory; that's always a possibility."

"How long?" Mitch repeated harshly.

The doctor drew a breath. "It's really remarkable in many ways, Mr. Mitchell. Today is the anniversary of your accident. Christmas Eve. December 24—1988."

It was worse than a shock, and no amount of bracing could protect against it. He couldn't breathe for a moment, and some wild, primitive cry of protest tangled violently in the back of his throat. Lost. Nine years lost forever. Nine years stolen while he slept. The whole world had gone on without him, seasons changing and lives lived and . . .

"Kelly," he whispered.

One

It was just a few days into February when Kelly opened her mail and found the clipping. There was no note, and no return address on the envelope; the postmark was smeared and unreadable. The clipping was from a major East Coast newspaper, but the article was a small one. The author of the piece seemed to feel that his information was newsworthy only because the situation was a bizarre one, and he clearly relished the odd coincidence of dates.

On Christmas Eve, 1979, John Mitchell had been involved in a car accident that had left him in a coma. On Christmas Eve, 1988, he had awakened, as if from a night's sleep.

There was more, a few bare facts. A battery of tests on Mitchell had found no brain damage. Intense physical therapy over months had repaired the ravages of the long coma, and doctors were astonished by his progress. There had been no setbacks, and the medical staff at the hospital was confident enough to anticipate no future ones.

For a long moment, as she stared at the clipping, Kelly felt nothing except distant shock. Then, as if a dam had burst inside her, a complex tangle of emotions washed through her. Happiness, relief, guilt, bitterness, anger. And last of all hurt, because Mitch had come out of the coma more than a year before.

He hadn't contacted her in any way.

She tried to be fair, reminding herself that he *could* have looked for her and simply not been able to find her. After all, she had learned to cover her tracks with all the caution of a hunted animal. The past ten years had taken her far from home, and no one who had known her then would even think to look for her in Tucson.

Kelly rose from her chair, the clipping still in her hand, and went to gaze out the window. The desert scenery was still unfamiliar, but already she was feeling the urge to move on. She had stayed here too long, months now. Her awareness of her surroundings was growing more intense, the urge to look over her shoulder stronger with every passing day.

It certainly was time to move on.

The phone rang, and Kelly crossed the living room of her tiny apartment and sat down on the couch to answer it. "Hello?"

"Miss Russell?"

"Yes?"

"Miss Russell, my name is Cyrus Fortune." His voice was soft and deep, and even over the phone the force of a strong yet curiously gentle personality was evident. "Your employers at ITC gave me this number; I hope you don't mind my calling you at home?"

"I don't mind. What can I do for you, Mr. Fortune?"

"Well, I'd like to offer you a job, Miss Russell. I understand that you enjoy traveling to different parts of the country to accept temporary assignments."

"Something like that," she murmured.

"I'm setting up a new company near Portland, Oregon, and I need a computer system designed. Are you interested?"

Oregon.

"Yes," she answered without giving herself time to think how odd the coincidence was. "My work at ITC is finished; I'm ready for . . . for a new challenge."

"Excellent. May I come to your office tomorrow morning and talk to you about it?"

"Of course. Would ten o'clock suit you?"

"Fine. I'll see you then, Miss Russell."

"Good-bye, Mr. Fortune."

She cradled the phone slowly and sat gazing at the clipping she held. Oregon. What a strange twist . . . Still, she would be moving even farther away from Mitch, not toward him, because he was, no doubt, in Baltimore. But it was better that way, she told herself. Because ten years was a very long time, too long to rekindle a flame snuffed out in pain and grief. She wasn't the girl John Mitchell had loved. And he hardly could be the man she had adored from childhood, not after what had happened to him.

Still, it hurt her to think of him waking all alone and facing so many shocks. The loss of years from his life. The loss of his eye. Keith's death in the accident. And the death of his father. Mitch and his father hadn't been on speaking terms for years before the accident, but the death of a parent is always a blow. The irony was that although Mitch had lost a great deal while he slept, he had gained the one thing he'd never wanted: the wealth of his family.

Kelly knew about that only because Hugh Mitchell had specifically requested that she be present at the reading of his will. Though he had never spoken to her in life, he had, after death, in a strange way acknowledged her place in his son's heart. Or, at least, so she had supposed. Because without explanation, and through careful arrangements making certain it hadn't cost her a penny in inheritance taxes, Hugh Mitchell had left her a house and property.

In Oregon.

She had speculated with a little bitterness whether he had specifically chosen that property to be her inheritance because it was across the country. Even though his son had been three years into the coma then, and not likely to recover according to the doctors, she had to wonder if Hugh Mitchell had still considered her a threat.

Kelly's first impulse had been to ignore the bequest, but she knew Mitch had spent time there as a boy and she'd been unable to cut that fragile tie to him. But neither had she been able to contemplate living there herself. Finally, she'd arranged with a realty company to rent the place and use the income for taxes and upkeep, and her family's lawyer kept an eye on the accounts. She had never gone to see the property, and though her lawyer had several times told her it was a valuable inheritance, she had refused to listen to appraisals or any other details.

Now it looked as though she would have the chance to see the place for the first time. She felt a little uneasy about that. She had avoided any place with ties for several years now, and it occurred to her that she might well be tempting fate by breaking her own rule. But what would be the harm? She'd stayed so firmly away from the Northwest that no one could possibly guess she would go there now, after all these years.

Still, it was something to think about. Kelly was on the point of rising when another thought occurred to her, this one definitely disturbing.

The clipping. Who had sent it to her? How could anyone in Tucson know of the connection between her and John Mitchell? And if the article had been sent from outside Tucson, then who had known just where to find her?

She stared at the bit of newsprint, conscious that her heart was thudding with the uneven rhythm she hated. The ache inside her was fear, and regret, and bitterness.

"Mitch . . ." she whispered to the silent room. "I should have waited for you."

"Well, Mr. Boyd?"

In his long career as a private investigator Evan Boyd had heard that terse question often. Clients tended to ask it when an investigation bogged down, and their voices grew more strained and harsh with every repetition.

But not this client. His voice had never altered, even though it had been nearly a year since he had first asked the question. A lot of control in this one, Boyd had decided. And, even more, the kind of relentless determination that few men could boast. It had served John Mitchell well.

"I have a lead," Boyd replied, but allowed his own misgivings to filter through his voice.

Mitch looked at him, and even though the investigator was no longer unnerved by that burning dark eye, he could feel the increasing force behind it. "A lead you don't trust?"

Boyd nodded, the perceptive response not surprising him since he had come to know this client. "It didn't come through the regular channels. Since she has a degree in computer science, I was checking into all the high-tech firms. If you remember, I warned you it could take a long time."

"I remember."

"Well, it *should* have taken a long time. But this morning I received a newsletter. The kind of thing some companies send out to their clients or employees once or twice a year. I can't explain how I got it, and the company—ITC, in Tucson—hasn't a clue either. They don't know me from Adam. And I wouldn't have known them; they weren't even on my list. ITC isn't strictly a high-tech firm. They're a small company, and they make toys, the garden-variety kind. Stuffed animals and dolls."

Mitch waited silently, his broad-shouldered, athletic body still and apparently relaxed behind the big desk. Boyd thought fleetingly of the man he had first met, a much thinner man who had been immersed in physical therapy in that private hospital; his driven determination to regain his strength and leave that place had, Boyd knew, worn out three therapists and astonished a number of doctors.

Curiously enough, the coma had left few signs of age on John Mitchell; and he actually looked younger now than he had when Boyd had first met him. The wings of silver at his temples had appeared only during the past year, and the black eye patch lent his lean, hard face a look of danger that was intensified by his invariable stillness.

"In the newsletter," the investigator went on, "was a small article about the company's new computer design program. They had hired a programmer on a temporary basis to set up the system. The programmer was Kelly Russell."

"Did you check it out?" For the first time there was a hint of strain in the deep, even voice.

"By phone, yeah. She was working there until three days ago. ITC says she's accepted another project, but they weren't willing to part with any of the details. I need to go out there and pick up the trail."

"You don't trust the information?"

"I don't like the way I got that newsletter out of the blue. Maybe it was just a fluke, but I don't trust flukes. Like I told you, I think she's running from something or someone, and I can't find out what. She seems to use her own name once she's settled in a place, but uses a false name to travel; that's what made it so hard to find her. And that's why it's so important that I go to Tucson and find out everything I can before the trail gets cold."

Mitch rose from the desk and stepped over to the window, gazing out at the city of Baltimore. Without turning, he said in a low voice, "You've gotten this close once before. Months ago, in Chicago. And lost her."

Boyd knew what he was being asked. And it wasn't only his professional pride at stake here, but a purely personal interest he had developed in this man and his search. In an equally quiet voice, he said, "I don't mean to lose her this time, Mr. Mitchell. I have contacts in Tucson; I'll pick up her trail."

There was a short silence, and then Mitch said, "Go. Report back the moment you find out anything. Call me any hour, day or night."

Boyd rose from his chair, then hesitated and drew the newsletter from the inside pocket of his coat. "I'll leave this with you," he said, leaning over to place it on the neat blotter. "There's a photo." Then he turned and left the silent office, knowing that John Mitchell would prefer to be alone.

The streets of Baltimore were busy. Mitch stood gazing out for a few moments, then turned and slowly went back to his desk. His desk. That still felt strange to him. He had made no changes in his father's office, and the executive board had made no change even though this room had gone unoccupied for years.

The old bastard had had the final word after all.

Hugh Mitchell's will had been a curious document. Dated just a few months before his death, it had clearly been written in the unshakable belief that his only son would survive to control the family holdings—no matter how long it took. The company had been set up meticulously, temporary control granted to the executive board and a group of trustees composed of accountants, lawyers, and financial advisers who had been required to work within a set of clear and unbreakable rules.

The result of all the care and forethought had been that Mitch had been able to step into his inheritance so smoothly it had caused hardly a ripple.

The bequest to Kelly had been a surprise, and since his father had left behind no remarks on the subject, Mitch couldn't guess what the intent had been, though he doubted it had been a positive one. At any rate, that promising lead had fizzled out quickly when it dead-ended with Kelly's lawyer; the man claimed he'd had no direct contact with her in years, and had no idea where she was. The realty company in charge of the property in Oregon had been just as useless.

Mitch sat down behind the desk, his gaze fixed on the folded newsletter lying on the blotter. His initial problems with depth perception due to the lost eye were virtually past now, and months of hard work had repaired the other results of his coma. He'd had literally to relearn many things, but there had been no brain damage to slow his progress, and at least he had the satisfaction of knowing that he was actually in better shape physically now than he had been ten years earlier.

Emotionally was something else.

He had discovered that the small shocks were, curiously enough, the ones that stayed with him. During the months of physical therapy at the hospital, Mitch had pored over magazines and newspapers in an effort to catch up with the world. The number of events he'd slept through was mind-boggling; some were minor, some major, and all of them made the world different.

Cars looked subtly different. Computers were everywhere, it seemed, as were satellite dishes and video stores. There were space shuttles now, making routine flights. Mount St. Helens had erupted. John Lennon was dead. There was a woman on the Supreme Court, and one had finally made it into space; England had a new princess and two new princes; a president had been elected, had survived an assassination attempt, and had served two terms. Baby boomers had come of age, and were making their presence felt in a number of ways. There had been a devastatingly long famine in Ethiopia, an earthquake in Mexico City, a tragic shuttle explosion, and terrorist insanity. The Statue of Liberty had gotten a face-lift, AIDS had become a terrifying epidemic, a Soviet leader named Gorbachev was charming the West, and they'd found the *Titanic*.

Mitch had had more than a year to begin absorbing the changes, but he still felt disoriented sometimes, out of step. It was one of the reasons he'd followed his father's wishes and taken his place in the company. At least he felt a sense of roots here, a sense of belonging, though he hadn't wanted any part of the company or his family's wealth.

What he wanted, more than anything, was to find Kelly. He didn't know what would happen then. He had loved her since she was fourteen years old, had planned his entire future around her, and now— And now. While he had slept she had lived through the days, and weeks, and years. He'd been told that she had lost her brother, her parents, and had given up on him.

He watched his hands reach out and slowly unfold the newsletter, then turn the pages until he saw her picture. An unposed shot, he thought, Kelly looking up from a computer keyboard as if she'd been startled. Her hair was shorter than he remembered, her face finer-featured, with adolescence well behind her. And there was something haunted in her eyes.

Why didn't you wait for me? He knew it was unreasonable, but the question echoed painfully in his mind, even though some part of him understood what her reasons must have been. She had been so young, and forced to bear so many shocks and griefs piled one on top of the other. It was natural, he told himself, that she turn to someone else eventually. She had been briefly married; Boyd had found that out quickly. Married five years after his accident, and divorced less than two years later.

Mitch didn't know—or want to know—about her ex-husband. The marriage had been registered in Texas, but if they had lived together there, Boyd hadn't been able to discover where. Since divorcing her husband, Kelly had been constantly on the move, living nowhere more than a few months at a time.

Was Boyd right? Was she running from something or someone? Or had Kelly simply lost so much that she was rootless, drifting through life? He didn't know, couldn't know, because he remembered only an eighteen-year-old girl; he was very much afraid the woman of twenty-eight would be a stranger to him.

The only thing Mitch was certain of was that he had to find her, had to see her and talk to her. She was all that was left of the future he had planned, the only link with the years that had been stolen from him. His mind told him she'd be different, changed by the life she had lived without him, but he had no emotional sense of those years passing, and his heart couldn't accept that she wouldn't still be the Kelly he had loved.

He had to find out. He didn't think he could bear it if he lost her too.

Two days later Boyd called, the satisfaction in his voice still mixed with a thread of doubt. "I finally got somewhere," he reported. "Her next-door neighbors in the apartment building are an old couple, very talkative. According to them, she's moved somewhere near Portland, Oregon."

"Find her," Mitch ordered, holding his voice steady with an effort. "Don't approach her at all, just find out where she is. Then call me."

"You've got it."

The house was more than a surprise. She didn't know quite what she had expected, but certainly not this huge, beautiful old house perched near the edge of a high cliff overlooking the Pacific. It was more than seventy years old, the realtor had told her, puzzled by her lack of knowledge, and they'd had no trouble renting it for weeks or months at a time during the past seven years.

Kelly could see why. The house was built of weathered stone, the style vaguely reminiscent of an English manor, with well-kept grounds and a spectacular view of the ocean. It had been built during an era when wealthy families had lived in luxury—and the Mitchells had been very wealthy. This "vacation retreat" was not a mansion by the standards of its day, but it was a large house on very valuable property and worth a fortune.

Before Kelly had inherited it, the house had been closed up and virtually abandoned for more than a decade. A year before his death, however, Hugh Mitchell had thrown an army of workmen into renovating and restoring it—apparently with the intention of leaving the property to Kelly.

The realtor, who had, as it turned out, been a very responsible and thoughtful caretaker, had presented her with an inventory of the contents of the house as well as a yearly appraisal from the insurance company. He had also hired a land-scape service to take care of the gardening, a cleaning service to take care of housekeeping, installed a very good security system, and had been selective about who he rented the place to.

Kelly certainly had nothing to complain about there. She'd told her lawyer that she wanted no income from the property, and that if there had been a profit from the rentals, it should be put back into the property. According to the realtor's itemized accounting, her wishes had been followed scrupulously.

But she didn't understand why Hugh Mitchell had left her the property at all. And the *way* he had, restoring the house and grounds, repairing or replacing all the furnishings, leaving the place ready to be occupied. It was as if he had fully expected her to live there, and that just didn't make sense. She had spent her few days wandering around the house and grounds, increasingly bothered by the situation.

Even the master bedroom had been decorated with a woman in mind.

Kelly was in the conservatory at the back of the house, gazing at white wicker furniture and lush green plants, when the doorbell sounded distantly. Since she was expecting the delivery, via her new boss, of a computer system, she wasn't surprised by the alien sound. She made her way back through the house, struck again by the quiet elegance of gleaming wood floors and antiques and beautiful old rugs.

She opened the heavy paneled oak door, expecting to see a delivery man with clipboard in hand and an inquiring look. And even though the newspaper article had at least prepared her for the possibility, she could feel the color drain from her face.

It was Mitch.

Taller than she remembered, his shoulders wider and heavier with maturity, a new look of strength and power in his stance. The gleaming dark sable hair had gone silver at the temples, but rather than making him look older, it, along with the black patch over his left eye, gave him an almost piratical air of danger.

"May I come in?" His voice was deeper than she remembered, slightly husky, and despite the prosaic request, she could hear the note of strain.

She stepped back wordlessly and opened the door wider, holding on so tightly to the ornate brass handle that she felt her nails biting into her palm. *Strangers*, she thought with the detachment that comes of total shock. *We're strangers.*

She pushed the door closed behind him as he came in, then led the way into the den, where a fire burned brightly in the stone fireplace. She didn't know what to say to him. Her legs felt shaky, and she sank down in a comfortable chair near the fire, watching as he slowly crossed the room and stood just a few feet away near the hearth.

"You knew I had come out of the coma." It wasn't a question.

Kelly answered anyway, her own voice holding tension. "I saw a newspaper article." She didn't mention that it had been only a week before.

Mitch slid his hands into the pockets of his dark slacks and looked at her steadily, giving no clue to his thoughts. He was wearing a black leather jacket over a dark gray shirt, and the somber colors made him look even more dangerous.

"I'm sorry," she said suddenly, almost blurting it out. There was a flash in the dark, watching eye, as if some emotion had surged inside him, but his face remained expressionless.

"Sorry for what, Kelly? That you didn't wait for me? I've seen all the medical records; I know what they told you." But there was something in his voice that didn't jibe with the words, something that might have been bitterness.

She gestured helplessly, then let her hands fall back into her lap. "The weeks turned into months. Years." Her voice was toneless now. "The only thing I could think of doing was to keep going, the way we'd planned. Finish college, get a job. And wait. But they told me you'd never wake up. The doctors seemed so sure of that."

"When did you give up on me?" he asked, the question somehow very important.

Kelly didn't want to relive that period of her life, but she had to answer him. "It was after Dad died. He outlived Mom by only a few months. Neither of them was the same after the accident. When he died, I realized I was alone. You'd been in the coma nearly four years. Everyone else was gone. And it hurt so much to keep hoping."

She drew a deep breath and met his gaze as steadily as she could. "It's easy enough to say that I would have waited if I could have known you'd come out of it. But I can't even tell you that's true. I don't know, Mitch. I don't even know if that would have made a difference. You had been so much of my life for so long, and when you weren't there anymore—"

"Someone else was."

Kelly could feel a new tension seep into her, and tried to keep calm. She didn't know if he knew of her marriage or was just guessing, but whichever it was, she wasn't willing to talk about that. Not to him.

She was increasingly aware of the strain of this,

the danger of exposing too many raw emotions. They were virtual strangers, but they shared too much pain, too many remembered dreams of the life they should have had. A large part of her shied away, urging her to cut whatever ties remained between them and finally end it, put it behind her once and for all. She was used to being alone now, and she knew all too well that she and Mitch could never go back to what they had been.

She rose to her feet, and somehow managed a distant, polite tone. "I just made fresh coffee; would you like some?"

After a moment he nodded slowly. He followed her as she went through the house to the kitchen, but it wasn't until she was pouring coffee that he made a comment.

"This place is different."

Kelly was standing on one side of a narrow, neat counter dividing the kitchen from a breakfast nook, and he on the other side. She set his cup down near him, realizing only then that she had automatically fixed his coffee with cream and no sugar, as he used to drink it. Unwilling to think about that, she responded to his comment in the same polite tone.

"I was told your father had the house renovated before he died. Any idea why he left it to me?"

"No." Mitch lifted his cup, watching her over the rim as he sipped the coffee. He chose not to mention that he noticed how she'd fixed it. "I went through some of his papers a couple of months ago, but whatever his motive was, he didn't write it down anywhere."

"You're running the business now?" She was determined to keep to unemotional topics.

"Yes. It seemed to be where I belonged—if anywhere."

Her cup clattered as she set it down on the counter. The tension inside her was winding tighter. There were too many emotions between them to be strangers, too much time between them to be anything else. Ignoring it wasn't going to help, she realized tautly. She was too aware of him, too conscious of all the things they had both lost. The distant echoes of pain and regret and bitterness were growing stronger, the limbo of numbness receding.

Mitch had come here for a reason; probably, she decided, he simply wanted to close the book on that part of his life and go on. That was reasonable, to want an ending between them. He had never been a man to leave anything unfinished. The way he was watching her made it obvious that he was just biding his time, almost as if he were waiting for her to say something.

Get it over with! she ordered herself. End it now, before it hurt too much, before she had to open a door closed in pain years earlier. She couldn't let that happen. Because she wouldn't be able to survive losing him a second time.

"Did you expect to find me here?" she asked flatly.

He nodded. "I knew you were here. I hired a private investigator a year ago to find you."

A year ago, soon after he'd come out of the coma. "Why? I gave up on you, remember?" She couldn't manage indifference, but was able—barely—to keep her tone without emphasis. "I made a life for myself without you. I buried you, Mitch, just the way I buried Keith and Mom and Dad."

Mitch set his cup down slowly, the intense gaze

still fixed on her face. A muscle flexed in his lean jaw. Then, suddenly, he reached across the narrow counter.

She felt a cool touch against her throat near the neckline of her blouse, but before she could stiffen or pull away, he had slipped one finger beneath the thin gold chain and drawn it toward him. As he pulled the chain taut between them, the diamond ring lifted from its resting place between her breasts and hung suspended. The stone caught the morning light and glittered brightly.

Kelly stared at the ring for an instant, then looked at him. For the first time he was smiling, though the expression was hardly more than a slight curve of his firm lips.

"I don't think so," he said quietly.

Two

For a long moment she didn't move, but only stared at him with her huge violet eyes. Then she reached up and caught the chain a couple of inches from his fingers, and pulled it away from him. The ring fell onto the smooth material of her blue blouse, and she fingered it for an instant before crossing her arms beneath her breasts.

"Don't read too much into that," she said stiffly.

Mitch knew he was walking a tightrope and that his balance had to be perfect. Even though he didn't *feel* the years that lay behind him—and between him and Kelly—he knew they existed. For her, the passage of time had been very real, and nothing he could say would be able to change it. He could only try to convince her that the past was no more dead and buried than he was.

He didn't try to fool himself into believing it would be easy. He knew all too well that he couldn't do for Kelly what the coma had done for him: make the years seem no more than a single painless night. Even if she hadn't buried him, she had mourned for what they had lost, and that was what set them apart right now.

Kelly had said her good-byes years before.

"What can I read into it, except the truth?" He held his voice steady and quiet. "You wouldn't be wearing that ring if you really had buried me. You still feel something for me."

She shook her head slightly, her shoulder-length copper hair gleaming with the movement. "The ring is habit, that's all. Like wearing a watch or earrings. Something you do automatically." She drew a breath. "I felt too much for too long, Mitch. One day I just stopped feeling."

"I don't believe that."

"It's the truth. What did I have to hold on to? Dreams? The dreams faded. You weren't there, and everyone kept telling me you weren't going to be. Ever. I finally believed them. I said good-bye to you, and I walked away."

"No regrets since?" He saw her almost flinch at the question, but even though he didn't want to hurt her, he refused to let it go. Let her go. She looked exhausted, the strain of this obviously affecting her strongly despite the control that kept her voice steady and unemotional, and that was the only thread of hope he'd found.

"What good are regrets? If it helps you to hear it, then, yes, I have regrets. A lot of regrets. But I can't go back and change anything. I can't change anything *now*. I'm sorry for what we lost, but I can't bring it back."

"Maybe not." All his consciousness was so totally fixed on her that he was aware of nothing else. "But I have to try, Kelly. I don't have a choice. For me, nine years passed in a night. I woke up loving you."

She felt a pain so sharp it took her breath for a moment, and when it passed, it left behind a dull ache. "Not me,'" she murmured. "Her. Don't you understand? I'm not her anymore. You don't know me, not now. I became somebody else while you were sleeping. I'm so different from that eighteen-year-old girl that we might as well be totally separate beings. The girl you loved is dead, Mitch. It's your turn to grieve . . . and get on with your life."

He was silent for a moment, his gaze so intense that it felt like an actual physical touch. Then he shook his head once, and said flatly, "No. I've already lost too much, all of it taken away from me while I slept, while I was helpless to stop any of it. But I'm not helpless now. I won't lose you too, Kelly. Not without a hell of a fight."

Ten years before, he had been the most determined, strong-willed man Kelly had ever known. Confident and assured, he had gone after what he wanted with a single-minded intensity that had utterly fascinated her. Their personalities had meshed perfectly then; he a leader and she willing to follow. She had, with the unconscious fervor of a young girl in love, begun molding herself into the kind of woman Mitch had wanted her to be; he was a strong man with a dominant personality, and in all likelihood she would have echoed his thoughts and opinions without forming her own.

But ten years stood between then and now, and for Kelly those years had been filled with events and emotions that had forever changed the woman she might have been. Looking back, she saw herself as weak and submissive, and with Mitch taken away from her, those flaws had become painfully evident. She knew now the price she had paid for her own lack of individuality.

Her maturity and independence had been hard-won, and she valued both now because the cost had been so great.

After a moment she said quietly, "What are you going to fight? Time? Fate? There's no villain, Mitch. No thief you can get your hands on. A drunk driver crashed into a car, after which lives took separate paths. If you came here thinking you could change that, you were wrong."

A muscle tightened in his lean jaw. "I can't accept that. I'll fight you if I have to. I'm not giving up on us." He hesitated, then drew a breath and added in a hard tone, "You owe me. You owe me time."

"I didn't take that away from you."

"No. But you walked away."

She wanted to walk away again. Just turn and walk away, order him out of her life. But he had, whether deliberately or not, laid bare her greatest regret—and her guilt. She had given up on him. She hadn't been strong enough, or hadn't loved enough, to wait no matter how long it took. It wasn't a rational guilt, and Kelly knew it, but knowing did nothing to lessen her feelings. She had lived with the guilt for more than five years, the only chain still binding her to the past.

She felt that she *did* owe him, that she should somehow atone for having failed him.

It had to be resolved, she knew that as well. The ring she still wore on a necklace was the constant reminder of everything and everyone she had lost one cold night, and until she made peace with herself she would never be able to put the ring—and the guilt—away. She had made so many mistakes in her life, and there would never be an opportunity to correct most of them. No matter what it cost her, at least she had to try to correct this one.

"Kelly?"

She looked at him, focusing on his face—a face almost as familiar to her as her own, even though it had changed in both stark and subtle ways. "I suppose in a way I do owe you," she told him steadily. "I owe you an ending. You won't be able to get on with your life until that chapter of it is closed."

"That isn't what I want, Kelly. I didn't come here to *finish* anything. You weren't a chapter in my life, you were the whole damned book. That hasn't changed."

"But I have. I didn't sleep for nine years . . . I lived. I got through the days one at a time. I buried my brother. I buried my parents. I finished college and built a career. I even . . . I even married another man."

"I know," he said flatly.

Kelly didn't want to let either of them dwell on that fact, and went on determinedly. "Then you know I'm not the girl you remember. I can't be. Pretending anything else would only hurt us both. It's over, Mitch. It was over years ago."

He slid his hands into the pockets of his jacket, his gaze never leaving her. After a moment he moved slightly, his shoulders settling as if he had braced them against something. "All right." His voice was even. "Maybe it is over. Maybe the girl I loved is lost to me, just like the years. But you still owe me. And I'm collecting on the debt."

"What kind of payment do you expect from me?"

"You said you owed me an ending. Fine. Give me that ending, Kelly."

"How?" she whispered.

"Let me find out for myself if the girl I loved is really gone. Is that too much to ask? A few weeks out of your life, a little time spent with me. Time without prejudice."

The guarded, wary part of Kelly resisted that, but she had already accepted the existence of a debt that had to be paid. "How could it be without prejudice?" she objected.

"Maybe it can't. But we can try. If it's over, I have to believe that. I have to feel it."

And then I'll have to say good-bye to you again. She didn't know if she could bear it. But she knew she had to. She couldn't be the one to walk away a second time.

With a faint shrug, trying to pretend this didn't matter to her, she said, "I have a career, and a job to do here. Your company's in Baltimore."

"I haven't officially taken over yet," he said. "After ten years, what's a few more weeks?"

A few more weeks. If the past pattern held true, she'd be safe here for at least that long. She'd managed months in Tucson before feeling any need to move on. But, someone had sent her that clipping, someone who knew she and Mitch were connected in some way. And now here she was in the Mitchell family's old vacation house. A house that was hers now—so it was a target. She hadn't been able to prove the damage done to her apartment in San Francisco had been anything other than vandals, but she knew.

For the first time in years, she wished that she had someone to turn to, someone to confide in. Not Mitch, though. He had borne enough pain without having to bear hers as well. She didn't want him to know about it, didn't want him to see her shame and fear. And if she hadn't been fairly certain she was safe here for a while, that there was no reason for him to know, she wouldn't have even considered his request.

"Dammit, Kelly—"

Realizing that she had been silent for too long, she managed another faint shrug before saying, "I agreed that I owe you."

Some of Mitch's tension seemed to ease. His tone was carefully neutral when he said, "I talked to your employer before I came here. Went to his office outside Portland. An . . . interesting man. He says you're going to work here in the house rather than at his company."

Kelly knew somehow that he hadn't changed the subject, but the tangent puzzled her. Making a mental note to ask Cyrus Fortune not to discuss her with anyone outside the office, she said, "That's right. He's sending all the equipment I need. The company's so new they're still getting organized, and I'll work much more efficiently if I'm out of all the confusion."

"So you'll be here all the time?"

"Probably."

He glanced away from her, looking briefly around the room in a considering way, then returned his gaze to her face. "Then it'll be much simpler if I just move into the house. This is a big place, plenty of room for two."

Kelly's first realization was that the statement was no spur-of-the-moment thought; he'd had this in mind long before he'd rung her doorbell. She wondered if he believed it would be so easy. Her impulse—and a very strong one—was to refuse to allow him to stay in the house. But she had learned to weigh her impulses carefully.

This impulse, she knew, was purely selfish. Too

guilty to push Mitch away and too afraid to cross the years between them, she'd been hoping for some painless solution—or absolution, some way of paying her debt without risking her emotions. But that wasn't right, it wasn't fair. Mitch wasn't at fault for what had happened to them, and he deserved peace just as much as she did.

"If that's what you want," she agreed finally. She saw the flash of satisfaction in his dark eye, and went on in the same mild but firm tone. "But there are ground rules, Mitch."

"Which are?" His voice was slightly wary.

"I'll be working long hours, and my job is important to me." It was the only thing she had made for herself, all she would have left when he was gone again. "You'll have to respect that."

He nodded immediately. "All right. I promise I won't disturb you while you're working."

"A cleaning service comes in once a week, but I expect you to do your share of work around the house."

"Agreed." He smiled very slightly. "I'd better warn you, though, I'm no better at cooking now than I was ten years ago."

Kelly refused to be charmed, but she couldn't help wondering how she could have forgotten how engaging his crooked half smile was. Keeping her voice dispassionate, she said, "There are cookbooks on the shelf by the pantry."

"I'll remember that," he murmured.

She remembered how he had been when announcing he would marry her—confident, assured, and never actually asking *her* about it. Not that she would have said no, but still, she knew now his kind of decisive—even masterful—attitude that had so intrigued her as a girl would run head-on into her independence ten years later. He was going to find that out, no doubt, but she had to make one last thing clear.

"And one more thing," she said quietly. "I've told you I'm different; you don't seem to want to accept it. I know that you see me as the only tie to those lost years, but—"

"Kelly—"

"Hear me out, Mitch." She held his gaze steadily. "If I've learned anything, it's that nothing is simple. I promised you an ending, but it may not be the one you want. If it isn't, don't think you can . . . can recreate the girl I used to be. No matter what happens, I won't be swallowed up by you. I've fought too hard to stand on my own two feet."

He was frowning now. "Is that what you think would have happened before? That you'd have been swallowed up by me?"

"It was already happening, before the accident." She conjured a faint, rueful smile. "You were strong, and I wasn't. You were so sure of yourself, so confident. Even arrogant." When he moved slightly, as if in protest, she nodded. "Oh, yes. But arrogance isn't necessarily a bad thing. Maybe your strength came from that. The problem was that there was so much of you and so little of me. And I never knew it. Until I was alone."

In that last simple sentence, so quietly uttered, was a world of stark emotion.

He drew a deep breath and let it out slowly. "I see we have a lot to talk about."

She knew that was true. What she didn't know was what would happen when the talking was done. And she already felt drained. She looked at their cold coffee on the counter and sighed. "That equipment I'm expecting should be here anytime.

Why don't you get your suitcases out of the car, and you can unpack."

He looked at her for a moment, and that crooked, engaging smile curved his lips. "You're that sure I came out here prepared to move in?"

As she moved around the counter toward the door that led into the hallway, she said dryly, "Wasn't I supposed to guess? Arrogant, remember? That hasn't changed."

Following her, Mitch felt a curious mixture of anxiety and fascination. Anxiety because he was beginning to realize she had changed a great deal— and fascination for the same reason. He knew without a shadow of a doubt that he was staying in the house only because Kelly had weighed the situation carefully and had decided to allow it; if she had decided against it, nothing he could have said would have budged her.

She wasn't hard, but there was a toughness in her now that had not been evident ten years before. It was part stubbornness, he thought, and part hard-won self-knowledge. The impulsive, emotional, pliant girl he remembered had grown into this thoughtful, wary, strong-willed woman.

It had been a shock to him, but not as great a shock as he had anticipated. Because even though he saw the changes in her, he *felt* a bond between them. He wasn't sure what that tie was composed of; right now the emotions were jumbled and confused. Pain and loss, guilt and bitterness, love and shared dreams, familiarity and strangeness, longing and regret. He felt it all, and he thought she did as well.

But she had gotten it into her head that everything between them belonged in the past, that they had no present together, no future. Her certainty of that was obvious. She'd made it all too clear that the time she was allowing them was only to prove to him what she already knew.

It had required all his will to keep himself from yanking her into his arms and convincing her she was wrong, but he was glad now that he had resisted that urge. It would have worked on the girl he remembered—but not the woman she'd become. He couldn't sweep her off her feet, couldn't carry her along on the wave of his own emotions.

And he was troubled by what she'd said about being swallowed by him. Was that true? She'd been so young when he realized he loved her, a fourteen-year-old from a close family with a protective older brother, and astonishingly innocent in so many ways. Had he dominated her without meaning to? His own emotions had been certain, and he had known she loved him—though, looking back now, he wondered why he'd been so sure.

"Damn," Kelly said mildly as she opened the front door. A delivery van was just pulling up in the drive. She glanced at Mitch, who had joined her at the top of the steps. "I'll have to show them where to put this stuff."

"No problem," he responded. "I'll take my things up and find a bedroom. You're in the master suite?"

She nodded. "You probably know the house better than I do. The beds aren't made, but the linen closet in the upstairs hall is stocked. It'll take me a few hours to get all the equipment set up; I want to get that done today."

He glanced at his watch and was somehow surprised to find it was still early afternoon. Then, as a delivery man came toward them with a clipboard and a harried expression, Mitch nodded an acknowledgment to Kelly and went down the steps toward his rental car. Her car was parked beside his, and he remembered that Cyrus Fortune had told him Kelly's standard employment agreement required that a company car be leased for her; since she moved from one part of the country to another with fair frequency, that made sense. She didn't have to concern herself with insurance or maintenance, yet made certain she had transportation.

He retrieved his suitcases and went back into the house, slipping through the doorway between two men carrying big sealed cartons. A glance showed him that Kelly had decided to set up her computer system in the large back parlor, where floor-to-ceiling windows provided plenty of light and a view of both the gardens and the ocean beyond.

Kelly was standing in the hall directing the delivery men, and as Mitch raised an eyebrow at her, she offered bemusedly, "He sent more than I asked for. I don't know what half this stuff is."

"I gather it's going to be a long day," he said lightly.

A hint of relief was in her brief smile. "Afraid so."

Mitch didn't like that look, because he knew where it came from. Despite her willingness to let him stay with her, she was wary and disturbed by his presence. But both the long months of physical therapy and his search for Kelly had taught him the value of patience, and he had no intention of letting his own fierce emotions push her farther away from him.

So his voice remained light. "Don't worry about

me. I'd like to explore the house and grounds. Do you mind?"

"No, of course not." Again, the flash of relief.

"Okay, then. See you later."

She nodded, and turned to speak to two men carrying in a labeled carton that looked like one section of a desk/computer work station.

Mitch went upstairs, looking around curiously as he noted the changes his father had made in the place. There weren't many structural changes that he could see, but the house looked much better than he vaguely remembered from his childhood. The floors had apparently been refinished, paneling and wallpaper replaced, and the furniture was different. There were five bedrooms with baths on the second floor, and an attic purely for storage occupied the top floor of the house. Mitch looked into each of the four rooms lining the hallway, then chose the one closest to the master suite.

He dropped his bags near the double bed, then immediately went back out into the hall and opened the door of the master bedroom. He didn't feel guilty at what she would likely consider trespass; if he was going to find out about the woman she'd become, he'd have to take every opportunity.

As soon as he walked into the room, he smelled Kelly. He'd noticed the scent before, downstairs, but with all his senses focused on her, it hadn't hit him like this. It was her perfume, so familiar that for an instant he could only stand breathing it in and remembering. Her fifteenth birthday, and his present had been her first bottle of "grown-up" perfume. He'd spent a long time choosing the fragrance, amusing the helpful salesclerk because he'd been so careful to find exactly what he'd wanted.

Oddly enough, the light, spicy scent with just a hint of musk suited her now far more than it had then. It was a little mysterious, quiet, and yet held the promise of things unseen, emotions untapped. She was still using the perfume he had chosen for her. Another habit? Or another tie to the past?

Mitch looked around the room slowly, and found it had changed more than any other part of the house. Heavy furniture and neutral fabrics and colors had been replaced by gleaming antiques, colorful rugs and wallpaper, and delicate fabrics. It was clearly and indisputably a woman's room, and yet a man wouldn't feel the least bit uncomfortable in it.

He stepped to the doorway of the bathroom and found it, too, had been remodeled. The old white tiles had been torn out and replaced by mosaic tiles in a muted pattern, the small window replaced by a three-sided bay window half wrapping a sunken tub that replaced the old claw-footed one and providing a spectacular view of the ocean. A glass shower stall had replaced the large linen closet. There were neat tile cubbyholes for towels, and an antique bureau was placed against one wall.

Now, that, Mitch thought, was definitely odd. Placing a bureau in a bathroom was not a standard decorating choice, but it was something Kelly had always preferred; since he had spent so much of his time with Keith during their high school years, Mitch knew that the small bureau in the Russell bathroom, which he'd asked about on his first visit to the house, had always contained underwear and sleepwear belonging to Kelly and her mother.

She could have moved the bureau in here since she'd arrived, but Mitch didn't think she had. That piece had the look of belonging, as if it were an integral part of the room. Coincidence? How could it be anything else? His father had been so adamantly opposed to the idea of his only son marrying into a working-class family—never mind the fact that he'd considered Mitch too young and Kelly *far* too young—that he'd taken no interest at all in finding out any of Kelly's habits.

Frowning to himself, Mitch turned around and studied the bedroom again. It was neat; that didn't surprise him. The small wooden antique jewelry box on the dresser was something he remembered because he'd given it to her. There was also a hairbrush and comb on the dresser and a bottle of perfume. A photo of her parents and brother in a silver frame.

He could still smell her perfume, as elusive as a dream.

After a long moment Mitch left her bedroom and returned to his own. He hardly noticed what it looked like, beyond a fleeting interest in more antique furniture. Unpacking occupied him for a few minutes, then he went out into the hall to the linen closet and found sheets and blankets. He heard the delivery men leaving, but ignored the urge to go down to find out how Kelly was coping with the equipment they'd brought.

He stripped the bedspread from the bare mattress and made up the bed, frowning to himself as he struggled mentally with the feeling of disorientation he'd been conscious of since first seeing Kelly. Not a new sensation, of course, but this time it was more than usually unnerving. The outward changes in her were minor ones, but just enough to make her seem slightly out of focus to him. Her hair was shorter and the coppery color more gold than he remembered; her face was more delicate, her violet eyes guarded, her smile brief and tentative. She seemed to him more slender, yet he didn't remember her breasts being so full or her legs so long.

It was like looking at a photo that was a little blurred, as if snapped during motion. His memories of her were strongly fixed in his mind, and none of them quite matched the reality.

He managed to shake off the disquieting feeling, knowing that only time could make past and present merge. Finishing in the bedroom, he decided to do what he'd told Kelly he would—explore the house and grounds.

In the car parked just off the narrow road, the man tapped his fingers restlessly against the steering wheel as he watched a delivery van pull out of the winding driveway and head toward Portland. When it was out of sight, he turned his gaze to the rooftop just visible in the distance through the trees. He hadn't had a chance to explore the place yet, because she hadn't left since he'd been watching.

And now she wasn't alone. He'd known she would come straight here once she found out her lover had survived the coma, and he wasn't surprised that Mitchell had come here as well. In a way, he was even pleased by that. At least now the bastard was out in the open instead of tucked away in some hospital.

He hated failure. He should have gotten to her long before this, but she seemed to know just when to run. It made him mad as hell. He'd been amusing himself so far, enjoying her fear, pleased each time she bolted like a scared rabbit. But it was time to teach her the final lesson now.

It was a matter of pride.

Kelly looked up as she heard a knock at the door of her new office, and wasn't surprised when Mitch poked his head in. But she was surprised to realize that it was dark outside, and she was surprised to feel a surge of some unidentifiable emotion as she looked at his lean face, the dark eye and rakish black eye patch and crooked smile.

"It's after seven," he said. "I dug out those cookbooks and tried my hand at baked chicken. How's your nerve?"

Despite herself, Kelly had to smile. "My nerve is fine," she said. "And I have a cast-iron stomach."

"Then I'll go put the rolls in the oven. Ten minutes?"

She nodded, and sat gazing at the closed door after he'd gone. Neatly arranged on its section of the three-piece desk, the computer hummed as it digested the basic programming she'd fed into it during the last hours. On a second section the printer was hooked up but silent, since it had as yet no work to do. In front of Kelly on the third section were stacks of files and graphs and reference books. All around the desk, in chairs and on the floor, were a number of boxes and cartons containing more equipment and supplies.

Kelly leaned back in her new and very comfortable office chair, lifting one hand to massage the back of her neck. The strain she'd felt since Mitch's arrival hadn't diminished, but she'd managed to focus her mind on the work, and that had helped at least a little.

I see we have a lot to talk about.

That was what she dreaded. The talking. Re-opening old wounds and feeling the pain again. All the questions he would no doubt ask about the last ten years, and the answers she didn't want to give him. She knew it was necessary, but she didn't want to relive the emotions. And she didn't want to feel new ones.

She had loved him as only the very young can love, without shadows, trusting and totally absorbed and completely without fear. She had loved him passionately, yet physical desire had been just awakening in her, the bloom of it shyly unfolding and unsure of itself. Mitch's desire had excited and intrigued her, but her starry dreams had included a white wedding dress and all the tradition that entailed; though he had made a number of decisions for both of them, he respected her wishes in that and agreed they should wait.

It was one of her regrets.

Shoving the memories violently away, Kelly began shutting the computer down. She neatened her desk as much as she could, then turned off the lamp and left the room. Mitch had turned on lamps through the house so that a welcoming light showed her the way to the kitchen, and she couldn't help but reflect on that small indication of not being alone. It was strangely comforting. And seductive. She'd been alone a long time.

He had set the small table in the breakfast nook rather than the more imposing one in the dining room. Everything was neat, and appetizing scents filled the bright kitchen. Mitch was transferring golden rolls from a baking pan to a linen-lined wicker basket, whistling softly. He'd shed his jacket and rolled the sleeves of his gray shirt up over his forearms, and despite his earlier comment, he looked as if he knew what he was doing.

As Kelly came into the room and heard him whistling—an old habit when he was absorbed in something—she winced and said lightly, "I never had the nerve to tell you before, but you're tone deaf."

He looked across the counter at her with a sudden gleam in his dark eye. "You're definitely not, as I remember. It must have driven you nuts."

"Sometimes," she confessed.

"Was I such an ogre that it took nerve to tell me?" His voice was as light as hers had been, but underneath was a very serious question.

"No. I just didn't have much nerve."

He continued to look at her for a moment, then said, "I found a bottle of wine. It's on the table. If you'll pour, we can dig into this feast."

The wine was excellent—and the feast wasn't half bad. He might not have had much practice at cooking, but it was obvious Mitch could follow recipes. Kelly wasn't lying when she told him the food was delicious. And even though she hadn't felt very hungry, her appetite increased with the first taste of tender baked chicken. She ate more than usual.

She felt some of her tension ease as well, but whether that was due to the food, the wine, or Mitch's easy and casual company, she couldn't have said. Sticking determinedly with the present, he asked her about the job she was doing for Cyrus Fortune, and seemed interested in the work.

Prompted by his intelligent questions, she explained what was involved in writing a wide-ranging program for a company. He was most intrigued by the realization that by the time she finished her job, Kelly had to have learned virtually every function of the company.

"It's really that involved?" he asked as they were finishing dessert—peach pie he'd discovered in the freezer.

"Sure. For instance, it's easy to write a basic accounting program, but if the company involved has half a dozen sources of income, it gets a lot tougher. And if that same company has an eye to the future and wants to project their earnings years in advance, that's another complication." She shrugged. "Fortune's company is definitely going to be a challenge. From what I can gather so far, he's forming the Portland office as a base to consolidate a dozen different companies across the country. He wants a network, a solid link tying everything together."

"Funny, he didn't look like an entrepreneur," Mitch commented.

"Neither did Colonel Sanders."

"Touché." Mitch smiled at her easily. "Why don't you take your coffee into the den while I clear up in here."

"You cooked. I should—"

He shook his head. "Let me take over kitchen duties for a while. I could use the practice, and you're going to have your hands full writing Fortune's program."

Kelly wasn't sure if Mitch was trying to make points or if he really did want to practice his domestic skills. *You're getting cynical,* she thought, and wasn't happy about that. She'd learned not to take anything or anyone at face value, but her own wariness sat uncomfortably on her shoulders.

"Kelly? You look tired. Go into the den." His voice was suddenly gentle.

How long had it been since anyone had cared that she was tired? Too long, because it affected her too strongly. Nodding, she left the table, carrying her coffee back through the house to the front den. The fire had been rebuilt, and the room was warm and cozy. She could dimly hear the wind whining outside, and it was a lonely sound that disturbed her. The wind always grew stronger at night, and she'd thought she was getting used to it, but tonight the sound was unnerving. Ignoring the television in one corner, she went to the stereo nearby and put in a cassette tape of soft music.

She looked at the couch for only a moment before kicking off her shoes and curling up in the big armchair near the fireplace. She was tired. Half listening to the quiet music, she gazed into the fire and tried to ignore the sneering taunt that had begun running through her mind during dinner.

You can't go back . . . can't go back . . . can't . . .

Somebody had wisely said it. You can't go home. Can't go back to your past. The problem was that Kelly's past had come to her. Too much had been left hanging between her and Mitch, left unresolved, incomplete. And she could no longer fool herself into believing that her own feelings had died. Perhaps she *had* buried them when she'd said good-bye to him, but he had walked through her front door, bringing the feelings with him.

They were inside her now, a little alien because those old emotions were being filtered, passing through the experiences and awareness of ten years. She had been conscious of them while she had talked casually to Mitch, trying not to let herself feel but helpless to prevent it.

Though lovers be lost, love shall not . . .

The next line of that suddenly remembered poem was just as vivid in her mind, and she felt the stark truth of it for the first time.

And death shall have no dominion.

Mitch had cheated death, awakening from a coma that medical science maintained he should not have awakened from. He had come looking for her across the years and the miles, determined to find what had been lost, mend what fate had broken. And she had offered him the chance, wary and convinced she felt too guilty to refuse what he asked of her. But it wasn't guilt, not just that.

"Did you love him?"

She turned her head slowly and looked at Mitch, everything inside her stilled. He had come into the room quietly, and now stood just a few feet away, gazing at her with a hard look around his mouth, a tightness in his jaw.

"I didn't think I'd want to know," he said in the same roughened voice. "But I do. Did you love him, Kelly?"

Three

Kelly looked away from him and returned her gaze to the fire. She felt curiously still inside, as if everything had stopped to wait for something. "It isn't that simple," she said finally.

"Isn't it?" Mitch moved to the chair on the other side of the fireplace and sat down, leaning forward with his elbows on his knees, staring at her with the hard, almost driven intensity that made her feel wary. "It should be, Kelly. It should be that simple."

She could feel his gaze, but continued to look at the fire. "No. It isn't. I—I needed someone, Mitch. I was alone, and I didn't know how to be."

"So you didn't love him?"

Kelly set her coffee cup on the small table by her chair, then looked at him. The stillness was giving way to a confused tangle of emotions, and she was trying to sort through them, trying to find only the bleached white bones of a truth that would satisfy him.

"I don't know. I felt a need for him. An emotional need. He had a kind of aura. Purpose, strength. He said he wanted to take care of me, and I needed that."

Mitch looked down at the hands clasped before him, and she could see that his knuckles were white. After a moment, steadily, he asked, "What happened?"

She rested her head against the high back of the chair, trying to think of an answer. She didn't want to lie, but even less did she want to tell him the entire truth. "I suppose . . . I realized I had to learn to take care of myself." Which was, after all, true enough. "That I had to stop depending on others to make me feel worthwhile."

His gaze lifted to her face, and his voice was grim when he said, "Worthwhile. How could you not feel worthwhile? Was it really that bad, Kelly? Did I and your family smother you that much?"

She was relieved that he hadn't pressed her for more detail about her marriage, but the question he asked was nearly as difficult to answer. Shaking her head slightly, she said, "I don't blame you or my family. That was one of the things I had to face up to, that it was my own fault . . . not the fault of an old-fashioned family or an assertive fiancé. No, the flaw was in me, Mitch. Nobody told me I *had* to be the kind of woman my mother was—so totally devoted to her husband and children that nothing else was important to her, so wrapped up in them and their lives that she lost her own individuality."

"I loved your mother," Mitch said, and the statement was both wistful and defensive.

"So did I. She was easy to love. And she was happy with her life, I know that. She was a loving, gentle, motherly woman; that was her greatest strength. And her greatest weakness. She poured so much love into her family that when Keith died it was as if a part of her had been cut away. Twice as bad, because she thought of you as a second son. Her family was wounded, and she bled to death."

Kelly drew a breath, and her voice was soft when she went on. "That was the kind of woman she was, the example I had in front of me all my life. It was natural for me to want to be like her, to consider the wishes of everyone I loved first and ignore my own. The problem was that Mom was the genuine article. I was just a pale copy. I didn't know what I wanted or needed, I never stopped to think about it. It never occurred to me that I had to learn to value myself before I could expect to be valued by others."

"*I* valued you," Mitch said intensely.

She'd had ten long years to think about it, and now her response was immediate and certain. "What you valued was my reflection of you, Mitch. And my willingness to be what you wanted. It couldn't have been anything else, because there was nothing else there."

"Kelly—"

"Think about it. You have to see it's true. I'm not saying you were conscious of your reasons. But love *comes* from need. What did you need from me?"

"You tell me," he said a bit tightly. "You seem to have it all figured out."

Ignoring the sarcasm, she said, "Your own family was anything but traditional. Your father was a domineering man, and your mother refused to be dominated by him. She wanted a career, friends apart from him, travel. And maybe it was unfortunate for all of you that she was just as strong-willed as your father. They fought right up until the day she left. Not six months later, you met Keith in high school, and his very traditional family adopted you in spirit."

Mitch was staring at his hands again, silent, a little pale. Kelly knew how hard it had to be for him to hear this, but she had to make him understand that even the past hadn't been exactly as he remembered it.

"We were so different from your own family. There were no bitter disputes in our house, no struggle for authority or confusion about what we were supposed to be. My parents had been together since they were sixteen years old; they'd decided on the roles a long time before. There was Keith, so secure in his world, loved and supported."

"And you," Mitch said in a low voice.

She nodded. "And me. I was just a kid, Keith's little sister. It was years before you really noticed me, and by then I adored you. I would have done anything to please you, even go on pretending I could be the kind of woman my mother was. That's what you saw in me, that willingness to be whatever you wanted me to be. Unlike your father, I accepted you just the way you were. Unlike your mother—"

"You don't have to say it." He sighed roughly, lifting his gaze at last to look intently at her quiet face. "What would have happened if we had gotten married, Kelly? If there'd been no accident."

Her hands rose slightly in a helpless gesture and then fell to her lap. "I don't know. Maybe nothing drastic. I might have grown up slowly, and you might have accepted me. Both of us could have adjusted. Or I might have been like so many women who look around in their thirties or forties and realize they have gone from being somebody's daughter to somebody's wife to somebody's mother, and they rebel. But I would have changed. I had to change, Mitch; it was inevitable. The accident and everything that happened after just made the changes come faster and more painfully."

"And now? You said you didn't know what you wanted or needed then. Do you know now?"

Another tough question. "Partly. I know what I don't want. I don't want to live through somebody else. To do what others expect me to do, be what they think I should be. I have to make my own choices, my own decisions. I have to control my own life, at least as much as any of us can."

"Kelly . . . I never intentionally tried to make you be something you weren't."

"I know." She looked at him steadily. "But you needed me to be something I wasn't, Mitch, and I felt that even then. I'm not blaming you; none of us can help our needs. And I was more than willing. I needed the security of a dominant partner because I was afraid of being alone, afraid of testing my own strength. What you have to understand is that I don't need that anymore. Or want it. And if your needs haven't changed, you won't find what you're looking for in me."

The click of the tape deck turning itself off was loud in the silence. Then, quietly, Mitch said, "I have changed, Kelly. I went to sleep in my twenties and woke up in my thirties. I lost an eye, my best friend, and the girl I was going to marry. The father I never made peace with has died. The whole world is so changed, not an hour goes by that I don't notice I'm out of step in some way. I'm rebuilding my life almost from scratch. How could I not be different?"

Kelly felt the pressure of hot tears behind her eyes, and her throat was aching. His voice had held steady, the eloquent words not a plea for compassion but a simple statement of what had happened to him. It moved her in ways she hadn't expected, made her feel his losses as keenly as she felt her own. For the first time, she was aware of her guard wavering, as if one or both of them had taken at least a small step to begin crossing the years between them.

She didn't know what would happen when—or if—they met again somewhere in the present. Every step would be tentative and painful, the way carrying them across old hurts and new, unexplored ground. But if they did finally meet, it would be as two adults who had learned to see each other clearly.

Kelly was afraid of the distance yet to be crossed. She was afraid of opening old wounds. But she couldn't deny even to herself the knowledge that the attempt was something she couldn't walk—or run—away from.

Finally, she swallowed the ache in her throat and said, "Neither of us is the person we were ten years ago. And we can't go back. The only way is forward."

Mitch drew a short breath. "I want you to understand that even though I'm not sure of everything I need yet, I do know it isn't what I needed ten years ago. I guess I wanted security just like you did, but in a different way. I'd seen my parents fight a tug-of-war all my life, and it was like being caught up in a storm of bitterness that never died. I suppose that I believed if only one controlled in a relationship, there'd be peace."

"You don't think so now?"

A faint, rueful smile tugged at his lips. "I think control is an illusion we build to protect ourselves, and the larger we try to make that circle, the weaker it gets. We can't control our own destinies, much less someone else's. And even the illusion is so fragile, any change can destroy it.

"I don't want peace, either, not that kind. Not the false calm of one person's individuality sacrificed. I saw the struggle my parents went through for years, and you've made me see what my own blindness would have done to us. But there must be a compromise between the two. There's a balance, Kelly, and that's what I hope we can find. A partnership. I don't want us to be together because either of us is afraid. We have to be whole *before* we can share what we are with each other."

She knew what he meant. For years she had felt incomplete. Finding her own strength had helped, but there was still, at the core of herself, some uncertainty she didn't want to examine too closely.

"Are you whole?" she asked hesitantly.

"No." His answer was immediate, his voice steady. "There are still too many pieces missing. I have to come to terms with what I lost and how it's changed me."

In a sudden moment of understanding, she said, "You knew that before you came here. You knew what we had was gone. But I am the only emotional tie left to your past."

Mitch nodded, his gaze holding hers. "I've been thinking about it ever since we talked earlier today. And in a way, you were right about that. But so was I. It's something I have to feel, to accept. I can't go forward until I stop looking back. I can't reconcile past and present yet. You're the only one who can help me do that, Kelly."

"So that's what you need from me now?"

He hesitated briefly. "Yes. For right now. You've had ten years to find yourself, and I think you have. But for me, the present's blurred because there's too much of the past standing in the way. I do have to close that chapter of my life and put it behind me."

He had, she realized, carefully talked about what he hoped they could find together before saying anything about closing the door on his past. It seemed he still believed she would be a part of his life no matter what he came to understand about the past and the present.

Her eyes still on him, she said, "You think that by spending time with me you'll be able to do that."

"Yes."

It was what she'd already agreed to, but the strain of this first day had stretched her nerves taut, and there was a request she had to make. "Mitch, I know we have to talk about all this. For both our sakes. But I—I don't think I can take much more right now. Can we try to forget about the past for a while? Tackle it slowly?"

The crooked smile softened his hard face. "I'll do my best."

She uncurled from the chair and found her discarded shoes, then got to her feet. "It's been a long day," she murmured, wryly aware of the understatement. "I'm going to bed."

"See you in the morning," Mitch said.

Kelly went up to her room. Without thinking very much, she closed the wooden shutters at the windows around the sunken tub in her bathroom and took a long, hot bath, trying to soak away the tension. When the water began to cool, she got out and dried off. She dressed in a fresh night-gown from the small bureau, then opened her bedroom window an inch and crawled into the big four-poster.

The wind outside whined softly, and the ocean was a distant roar, rhythmic and soothing. She turned out her nightstand lamp and lay watching the moving shadows in the room as the trees outside filtered the moonlight.

Mitch had changed, she thought, but the enormous strength in him had withstood the years and all his losses. It was an emotional strength, the inner toughness of someone who had grown up in the midst of other strong personalities; he had learned young to assert himself, to avoid being overshadowed. That quality in him had awed her once, but now she simply respected it because she'd found her own brand of strength.

He seemed more patient now, more willing to listen to what she had to say. And more willing to talk about his own feelings. She thought the last year had changed him in those ways. Not so much the coma itself, but the shock of awakening.

He'd said the past and present were blurred for him, and in a way she was coping with the same problem. The last years had taught her to resist the kind of man Mitch had been, to protect her individuality fiercely, and that lesson had been a hard one; she would never again be weak or submissive. If he had come back into her life with the manner she remembered, she would have ignored her own unresolved feelings and ended it between them no matter what he said.

But he hadn't demanded, hadn't tried to overpower her or make light of her objections. He hadn't tried to impose his will on her; he had used reason, not domination. He seemed to her just as strong-willed as he had been ten years before, perhaps even more so, yet he was also watchful and quieter and more self-contained. She didn't quite know how to react to this Mitch, her past knowledge warning her to keep a distance between them even as she was conscious of feeling drawn to him.

She had never looked at him through a woman's eyes, not really. Not until today. And today he was different.

Kelly turned onto her side and stared toward the window, trying to relax, to stop thinking. It occurred to her only a long time later as she was drifting off to sleep that it wasn't just her mind and emotions that were drawn to Mitch. With all the tensions between them, she hadn't realized how her body had reacted, how she'd been vibrantly aware of his every movement.

Except for when he had lifted the gold chain she wore, they hadn't touched at all. Yet she'd felt every glance, felt his voice like some strange, taut vibration in the air that brushed her skin softly. New, unfamiliar, and unnerving feelings. And those feelings followed her into sleep, prompting dreams like none she'd ever had before. . . .

He drew his thick jacket tighter and turned up the collar, mildly annoyed by the coldness of the wind. From his position in the lower level of the garden he could see the house clearly, had watched lights going out downstairs. She'd taken a bath, he thought, but had closed the wooden shutters so he couldn't see. Modest little bitch. They were all like that, though, at least to hear them talk.

Protesting the lights being on, acting uncomfortable about dressing and undressing around him. Trying to hide from him even when they were his to look at as much as he damned well pleased.

Then her bedroom light had gone out, and he had seen the dim glow in another bedroom, realizing that the two in the house weren't sharing a bed yet. The very thought of the bastard in her bed made bile rise in his throat, and he spat into the bushes angrily. Ghosts were impossible to kill, but Mitchell was flesh and blood.

He stared up at the bedroom window, barely able to make out a shadowy form, then glanced toward the cliffs. He'd looked the place over thoroughly, and knew there were wooden steps leading down to the narrow strip of sand. After a while he leaned against a tree and watched the window, waiting patiently for that other watcher to go to bed.

Mitch stood at his bedroom window, staring out into the shifting landscape. The trees tossed restlessly, blown by the fractious coastal winds, and now and then he caught a glimpse of the dark gleam of the sea. The hardwood trees were naked branches moving eerily, and the pines whispered and sighed as they swayed. It was a lonely sight.

He found it difficult to trust sleep now, to relax and give himself up to it. The therapists had told him that was natural and that one day he'd be able to close his eye without feeling the dark stirrings of fear. Doctors had assured him that there was no likelihood of his slipping back into a coma. Not likely at all, they'd said with quick smiles.

But then, it hadn't been likely that he would ever awake from the coma at all.

He hadn't wanted even to close his eye in those first days, his resistance almost obsessive, until sheer exhaustion had taken the choice out of his hands. It hadn't gotten any easier in all the months since. The sensation of drifting toward unconsciousness, so pleasant for most people, was for him a stoic leap of faith. And each time he opened his eye, his muscles were braced, the single thought in his mind like neon.

Just a night. Please, just a night . . .

Even now he found it impossible to sleep through the night. He woke often, peering in the darkness at the digital watch whose red numbers kept track of time and day and month and year. A reassurance that would allow him, minutes or hours later, to take the leap yet again.

So little control. That had been hardest to accept, that even his own mind and body could betray him. That fate could step in without warning and steal years. And that there was not one single, damned thing he could do to stop it.

That was why he had so quickly seen and understood what Kelly had talked about. Ten years earlier he had sought control in order to avoid the bitter struggles he remembered so vividly. Perhaps unconsciously he had fallen in love with Kelly because she'd been so young and adoring, so pliant to his wishes, because, as she'd said, he needed that. But now he knew only too well what an illusion control was.

More, he was beginning to realize that even the illusion was a cheat when it surrounded two people, and a twisted one at that. He would have fought like a tiger to avoid even the suggestion of surrendering his own individuality to another's, yet he had—unconsciously—expected Kelly to do just that. To be swallowed up by him, to live through him.

It made him a little sick now to think of it.

He stood by the chilly window, still dressed because he wasn't yet prepared to risk giving himself over to sleep, staring out without seeing because he was looking back at the past and inward at himself and his life. It came to him slowly, with a distant shock, that his father had been terrified of losing his mother. A naturally possessive and willful man, he'd seen his wife's need for independence as a threat, and had either loved too much himself or trusted in her love too little. Perhaps both. Rather than risking losing her, he had held on tighter, demanding that she belong only to him.

She had fought him for years, and Mitch realized now that the struggle had gone on so long only because his mother *had* loved his father, and *had* sought to preserve her marriage without losing herself. In the end, unable to live through her husband as he demanded, she had chosen, painfully, to live without him. She had told her son that he could come to her as soon as he was of age; Hugh Mitchell would have fought tooth and nail if that battle had gone to court.

She had died in a plane crash two months later.

With her gone, Mitch had launched a war of his own, blaming his father and rebelling at the slightest show of authority. He hadn't understood the complexities of relationships then, and had seen only the results of his father's domination. Now, looking back, he realized that it had been largely a case of history repeating itself. Hugh Mitchell had held on tightly to his son out of fear, and Mitch had pulled away all the harder. Until, finally, the decision to marry Kelly had caused the final break between them.

Love without trust. The difference between holding a hand and chaining a soul.

His father must have been a lonely man.

Mitch leaned his forehead against the cold glass and stared out at the bleak, alien landscape. How close he'd come to repeating his father's mistakes. And he would have, had not fate intervened.

I was alone, and I didn't know how to be.

But she had learned how to be. After her brief marriage. There was, Mitch thought, more to that than she'd told him. He'd heard it in her voice, but hadn't been willing to probe because it had been like a knife inside him to hear her say she'd needed another man. But he'd have to hear it sooner or later; he'd have to listen and deal with his own feelings. That was part of the past he had to accept, part of who Kelly was now. Another man had been her first lover. Her husband.

He had no right to be jealous, but he was. No right to feel bitter and betrayed, but he did. He still was enough of the possessive, willful man he had been to feel the violence of those emotions even while he recognized them as unreasoning. And because she *was* the last tie to all he'd been, he had to fight an even more desperate urge to hold on too tight, to demand of her how she could have given herself to another man. To blame her for the pain he felt.

The emotions were raw inside him, a jumble composed of past and present. He didn't know where one left off and the other began, or if there could even be, in the end, a division between the two. The only thing he was certain of was that his need for Kelly was far greater and infinitely more complicated than it had been ten years earlier, and that if he were able to win her love this time, it would happen only once he mastered his own innate possessiveness.

And that was going to be very difficult for him. He had accepted that control was an illusion, but he had lost so much that the fear of losing her was something he couldn't bring himself to contemplate.

Yet he had to let go. Let go of the past. Let go of Kelly. He had tried to chain her then, and fate had stopped him. He had to stop himself from trying to chain her now. If she could learn to love him again . . . he had to learn to trust that love enough to hold only a hand.

Not a soul.

It was three in the morning when he roused himself and glanced toward the waiting bed. But he didn't move toward it, and after a moment he returned his gaze to the wind-tossed trees that teased him with glimpses of the ocean.

He wasn't ready. Not yet.

"Good morning."

Mitch looked up from his work to see her standing just inside the kitchen. Wearing jeans and a dark blue cowl-neck sweater, her bright coppery hair pulled back away from her face and tied with a ribbon, she was lovely and a little wary, but less strained than she had been the night before.

Perhaps it was her sudden appearance, or the demons he had wrestled with in the night, but for one fleeting instant he saw her clearly, without the blurring of past images. He saw intelligence in her violet eyes, sensitivity and vulnerability in the curve of her lips, stubbornness in the delicate line of her jaw. He saw the slender figure of a woman who moved slowly and gracefully, shoulders almost unconsciously braced, something of vigilance in the tilt of her head.

He saw a woman who had lost a great deal, perhaps much more than he knew. No girl now, but a woman who had survived.

And in that brief moment he felt a desire for her so strong it was almost like a blow. It was a feeling of stark necessity, a shattering tangle of physical and emotional needs. He wanted her not the way he had ten years earlier with a passion tempered both by her youth and by the arrogant certainty that she belonged to him; this was a need far more complex than anything he'd ever felt before—deeper, and grinding inside him. Not the male urge for possession, but a compulsive realization that she was half of himself and that without her he'd never be whole again.

"Mitch?" Faint color bloomed across her cheekbones, and her eyes skittered nervously away. "Is—is something wrong?"

With an effort that tore at him jaggedly, he pulled his gaze from her and looked down to watch idly as the spatula in his hand bent under the tightening force of his grip. *Too much,* he thought, *I'm feeling too much.* She'd seen it, and the apprehension in her eyes was plain.

Dear Lord, was she afraid of him? Afraid he'd resort to force, that he would attempt to overwhelm her with his own feelings?

He cleared his throat and carefully loosened his grip on the spatula, concentrating on reining his wild emotions. "Good morning. Ready for break-fast?" His voice held steady, somewhat to his surprise.

Kelly slid her hands into the pockets of her jeans, shaken by what she'd seen in his intense gaze and by her own instant response. These strange sensations, heat and tightness and a word-less yearning . . . they unnerved her.

"I usually don't eat breakfast," she murmured.

He glanced back up at her, the intensity shut-tered now, and where the old Mitch might have told her she was too thin and needed to eat more, this one merely said, with a faint smile, "Humor the cook."

She nodded and went to pour juice and coffee while he transferred golden pancakes from the griddle to plates. Kelly couldn't think of anything casual to say as they began eating, but she couldn't stop glancing up at him. He seemed different this morning, at least after that first oddly naked, sear-ing scrutiny of her. More . . . what? More with-drawn. As if his focus had turned inward.

And she felt peculiar, unable to stop herself from remembering her surprising dreams. She rarely remembered dreams, yet she vividly recalled those of last night. Some had been stunningly erotic, filled with shapes and images and colors and throbbing feelings. But the dream she re-membered most clearly had been different. It had been unnerving, threaded with tension that had built to a nightmare ending.

She had dreamed of Mitch as he was now, qui-eter and yet more compelling than he had been all those years before. He had been wandering through the house and grounds, walking along the beach at the base of the cliffs, and she thought he was looking for something he couldn't find. She'd wanted to tell him where it was, but hadn't been able to utter a word. Following him because she had to, because a misty bond connected them and it pulled at her irresistibly, she'd felt tense and restless, her heart thudding, needing to look over her shoulder but afraid to see what was behind her.

She had known somehow that if she could only catch up to Mitch and talk to him, whatever was behind her would go away and stop troubling her. But there seemed to be a measured distance between them, pulling the bond taut without snapping it, and all she could do was try not to lose sight of him. She wanted to walk faster, and couldn't, yet she could hear what was behind her getting closer, like her own shadow at her heels.

Breathless, troubled, longing, anxious for reasons she didn't understand, she had followed Mitch through the night, never able to close the distance between them. She'd heard quiet music that throbbed and a soft little chuckle that might have been the wind behind her, had seen the eerie shapes of trees bending and swaying, reaching out for her.

Then, as the stark gray light of dawn spread heavily through the air, Mitch had stopped on the edge of the cliffs, gazing out on the ocean, and she'd felt a jarring sense of urgency. She had to get to him, reach him, it would be her last chance. Behind her, hot breath on her neck, no, just the wind, it had to be the wind, and as long as she didn't look she was safe. Hurrying toward Mitch, seeing him turn and smile and hold out his hand. The lean, hard face and black eye patch, so dangerous, but not like the other one, he couldn't be.

She'd reached him at last, his hand touching hers, and then, behind her, the rushing of angry steps, the shadow overtaking, pushing.

Kelly had awakened with a cry trapped in her throat, her heart pounding, remembering vividly the sickening feeling of slamming into Mitch, both of them falling, the jagged rocks below spinning crazily as she closed her eyes.

"Does it bother you?" he asked suddenly, looking up from his plate.

"What?" she asked, startled, trying to push the stark images out of her mind.

Mitch made a slight gesture with his left hand toward the eye patch.

She wondered if he'd felt her glances, if her own restless anxiety had somehow touched him. "No. I—I got used to it in the hospital. It must have been rough on you though. Waking up."

"A shock at first." He shrugged. "It was the easiest thing to accept, really. I don't think about it much anymore."

Kelly smiled a little, forcing herself to be casual. "The patch makes you look piratical. Dangerous."

He considered that opinion for a moment, watching her with a faint smile but an unreadable expression. "Other men hardly notice it, as far as I can tell. Women definitely do. I just figured the interest came from a kind of maternal instinct. You know—a bird with a broken wing."

"It may be partly that," she said dryly, "but not all. Like I said, it makes you look dangerous, and a lot of women are drawn to that look. Pirates and rakes. Heartbreakers."

"Including you?" The question was light, but his gaze remained watchful.

She should have expected it, but she was nonetheless caught off guard. Compelled by something in him or by her own innate honesty, she said slowly, "I don't know. When I look at you, it isn't the patch I see. You're more impressive somehow than I remember. More complex. There's a stillness in you, a quiet that wasn't there before. Maybe I'm drawn to that."

Her own admission surprised her, but she didn't try to take it back. She was drawn to him, and for her own peace of mind she needed to understand why. Past, or present? Was it remnants of her guilt over having left him, or a deeper connection that had lain dormant inside her until she had been able to look at him through a woman's eyes?

Mitch seemed to hesitate, then said, "If that's what you see, it's deceptive. And elusive."

"Is that a warning?" She held her voice steady, even though something in his made her heart thud unevenly.

He half nodded, still looking at her. "I'm trying, Kelly. I'm trying to work through all this, I promise you. I don't want to be the kind of man my father was, holding on so tightly to someone I care about that I strangle them. But I've lost too much not to be afraid of losing again. It's something I have to fight all the time, that fear. I think that's why I haven't touched you."

She wanted to tell him that he *had* touched her, that she felt every glance, but her throat had closed up. She was aware of her pulse throbbing, of a strange, restless heat inside her, and the force of her own feelings bewildered her. And even though she'd never felt this way before, some instinct deeper than knowledge warned her that all the strength she'd fought so hard to gain would never be enough to fight this.

If she wanted to fight it.

Without a single physical touch he had made her aware of him, had made her feel the stirrings of longing. New, unfamiliar feelings that made what she had once felt for him seem like dim and distant echoes.

She was afraid. The fear had more than one level, like steps going down into darkness, and she couldn't make herself move from the topmost tread. She stood on the top step now, shaken by her own yearnings—and frozen by memories of pain. She hadn't felt these longings then, but she couldn't forget the pain and helplessness another man had taught her, couldn't make herself believe it would be different, because she could feel the intensity in Mitch, and the danger.

His low voice roughened. "I might not be able to let go once I touch you. I've wanted to hold you for so long that I'm afraid I'll hold too tight."

Four

Kelly didn't think he meant that literally. Then again, perhaps he did. Either way, she wasn't ready to find out. And she knew that his feelings were still unresolved; she'd heard that in his voice last night.

Did you love him?

After a long moment, holding on to every scrap of control she could manage, she said, "I'm glad you're trying not to be like your father. For your own sake." She couldn't bring herself to refer to the far more personal note he'd finished with, too wary to invite any discussion about touching.

Mitch didn't press her; he merely nodded and said, "I wanted you to know."

After breakfast Kelly retreated to her office with a cup of coffee and tried to concentrate on work. But she found herself distracted, sitting at her desk and gazing often through the big windows. It was overcast, chilly but not cold, and the morning mist seemed reluctant to retreat so that the very air had a leaden, gray look.

Like something pressing down insistently. That was probably it, she told herself. There was probably a low pressure front draped over them, and that was why she felt so jittery. She'd always been like a cat in her sensitivity to weather. Mitch had once told her he could always tell when a storm was coming because she'd get restless.

He'd known so well the girl she had been. He had seen her at her best, and at her worst. Long before she'd known what to do with makeup, he'd had ample time to study her unadorned features, and it had been Mitch—and only Mitch—she had believed when he'd told her she looked just fine in braces.

He had seen her in ratty jeans and flannel nightgowns, with curlers in her hair and a greenish mudpack on her face—and, she remembered, had withstood the shocks rather well. He had humorously endured all the wild fashion swings of her teens, his only demand that she leave her hair long and its natural color.

And before that, before he'd made up his mind to marry her, he'd been a part of her life. He had been fifteen when Keith had first brought him to the house, and Kelly had been eight. Since Keith had never minded his baby sister tagging along, and Mitch hadn't either, she had spent a great deal of time with them. She could remember Saturdays filled with learning to bait a hook or hit a curve ball or catch a long pass. She could remember Mitch reading to her when she was sick with the flu, and teaching her to play card games when she'd been miserable after having wisdom teeth extracted.

He had never teased her more than she could stand, either instinct or innate kindness telling him how far he could go without seriously hurting her feelings. And when he and Keith had discovered girls, he had continued to treat Kelly rather like his own baby sister. Fiercely resentful of his attentions to those older girls, it hadn't occurred to Kelly until she reached her own teens that she was jealous.

Thirteen, she reflected now rather wryly, was a melodramatic age for a girl. An age of trying so desperately to be grown-up that the results were, more often than not, ludicrous. An age of wild hairstyles cemented with hair spray, of junk jewelry, of makeup and perfume inexpertly applied. An age of fervent passions about clothing and music—and boys.

But when Kelly was thirteen, Mitch was twenty. Not a boy, but a man in college. She had tried so intensely to make him see that she was grown-up, terrified that he wouldn't realize until too late, after some other girl had married him. Oddly enough, she had never doubted that she was the one he really loved, if he'd only just *look* at her.

Some time after her fourteenth birthday, he had.

"Stop it," Kelly muttered to herself aloud, realizing that she'd gotten lost in the past. "That doesn't matter now."

But it did. She had known Mitch for twenty years, almost two thirds of her life, and that *did* make a difference.

She refused to let herself think about it anymore. For now at least. Forcing herself, she concentrated on her work, still getting organized as she put away supplies and arranged the reference materials neatly on her desk. She kept her mind on that and managed to stay occupied for several hours, but caught herself glancing toward the windows several times. Finally, giving in to the fidgety urge to move, she went over to one of the windows and stood looking out.

Even with the mist still clinging wispily to some of the tree branches and settling like a giant spider's dense web into low places here and there, the view was lovely. The house was set well back from the cliffs, and the sloping grounds had been divided into a bilevel garden. Nearest the house was a flagstone terrace with wrought iron tables and chairs, heavy stone planters filled with flowering plants not yet in bloom, and a low balustrade covered in shiny green ivy.

Between neat hedges, a flight of stone steps led down to the lower level, which was far larger and more sprawling than the formal terrace. There, flowering shrubs and ivy had been allowed to encroach on what had once been wide paths so that the area had the look of nature having reclaimed what man had attempted to master. The fact that the appearance was deliberate, Kelly thought, did not detract in the slightest from its appeal. Sections of lush green lawn were divided by groups of trees and thickets of shrubs and flowering plants, with stone benches placed here and there alive with ivy.

Gradually, the lower level gave way almost completely to nature as at least two of the paths led to the cliffs. The ground became sandy and rocky in patches, the muted roar of the sea louder and, if it was high tide, the crashing of waves against the base of the cliffs took on a new urgency.

I could live here always. The thought crept into her mind gently, and Kelly felt a wistful impulse to put down roots at last. It was, after all, the computer age, with the country connected by modems and FAX machines; she could work anywhere.

Without being aware of it, she lifted a hand to rest against the cool glass as she gazed out. A sense of motion caught her attention, and she watched as Mitch strolled across the terrace and took the steps down to the lower garden. He looked preoccupied, frowning a little, and Kelly felt a jolt as she recognized the expression he'd worn in her dream.

She tried to push that out of her mind, but the scene she was looking at, the leaden gray skies and pockets of mist, Mitch walking as if with a purpose he wasn't consciously aware of, triggered feelings of anxious urgency in her. As he moved away from her, he seemed to blur, and she found herself staring at her hand pressed to the glass.

Ten years ago. *Exactly* ten years ago, though neither she nor Mitch had mentioned it. She hadn't realized that until now, and perhaps he was unaware of dates. A hospital waiting room, bland and quiet, and a doctor's relentless, weary voice telling her that Mitch was never coming back to her.

"No." She heard her own voice, loud in the silence of the room, images in her mind a confused jumble of ten years before and a dream that had terrified her. She didn't stop to question her own compulsion; she knew only that she had to stop Mitch before he reached the cliffs.

She ran from the room, taking the quickest route through the conservatory and the French doors opening onto the terrace. Her heart was pounding as she hurried down the steps to the lower level of the garden, her eyes searching the way ahead to catch a glimpse of his pale ivory sweater. For the first time, she cursed the organized wilderness of the garden, because the only way to get to the cliffs was by one of the paths that twisted and turned through wet greenery with maddening leisure.

Then, finally, she took the last turn and saw Mitch. He was moving toward the wooden steps that led down to the beach.

"Mitch!"

He swung around to face her, the first surprise giving way to concern. "Kelly? What's wrong?"

She made herself slow down as she walked toward him, trying to calm the runaway pounding of her heart. It wasn't like the dream, of course, because two feet back from the edge of the cliffs was a low stone wall to protect the unwary. And Mitch was facing her; he'd surely react if there was something behind her rushing to shove them both over the edge, even though he hadn't in the dream.

"The steps," she said a little breathlessly as she reached him. "They aren't safe." Only as the words left her did she realize that was it. The dream made a kind of sense now, as did her urgent anxiety. The realtor had warned her that the steps needed repairing; there had been some beach erosion and the support posts had been damaged.

"I just remembered," she went on, stopping and glancing past him at the wooden railing that appeared deceptively sturdy. "The realtor who's been watching over the house for me said they needed to be rebuilt. He's going to send someone out next week. I should have warned you yesterday."

"I didn't go down yesterday," Mitch said, gazing at her with an expression she couldn't read. "But now that you're here, why don't we both go down? There's another way."

"Is there?"

He nodded toward the southern boundary of the property, where the low stone wall turned back inland and meandered through a healthy clump of ivy before being swallowed up by riotous hedges. "Just over the wall there. It's a fairly steep path, but solid. Are you game?"

Kelly hesitated. "I should go back to work."

"You've been working all morning," He glanced briefly at his watch. "Look, it's after eleven. Why don't we take a walk before the tide turns, then come back here and have lunch. You'll be fortified for a busy afternoon."

She felt the touch of a breeze, cool and damp, and realized that if she didn't walk off some of her restlessness she wouldn't be able to get any work done. Finding a logical explanation for her anxiety had helped, but she still felt a sense of pressure as if something were bearing down on her.

Nodding an assent, she turned with him and began walking toward the south boundary.

Mitch sent her a sidelong glance. "Storm coming?"

She grimaced faintly. "Does it show that plainly?"

"Not as much as it used to. You just seem a little edgy."

"I almost called the nearest weather bureau and asked if *they* knew there was a low pressure area around somewhere." Kelly conjured a smile, reminding herself that the simplest explanation was almost always the right one. She was jittery because there was a storm on the way, and that was that.

Smiling as well, Mitch said, "I always had a hell of a lot more faith in you than in the so-called professionals. I remember Keith saying once that even when you were a baby you kept everyone up nights if a storm was coming."

"If it doesn't hit by tonight," she said lightly, "I promise not to keep you up."

"Don't worry about that."

She looked at him as they reached the wall, hearing something in his voice but not being quite able to define it. The wall was a little less than waist-high, and she got over it quickly and neatly before he could offer to help. Then, staring down at nature's path to the beach fifty feet below, she reflected that he hadn't been kidding when he'd called it steep.

The path hugged the cliff, no more than a narrow walkway provided by a series of ledges almost like steps that dropped gradually to the beach. It would hardly be visible unless you knew it was there, which was why she hadn't noticed it before.

"Be brave," Mitch said with a smile, obviously noting her hesitation. "I promise these steps don't need rebuilding." He reached out a hand and took hers firmly. "I'll lead."

Kelly couldn't have protested even if she'd wanted to, and followed as he began leading the way. She was very conscious of the warm strength of his hand and the fact that this was the first physical touch between them. And her reaction to that bothered her. The unfamiliar feelings she'd been aware of became stronger at the touch, but there was more this time than nameless longings and a strange liquid heat; she'd felt an instant sense of rightness.

Like a connection made. A loop sealed.

"All right?" Mitch asked, pausing on a step below her to make sure she was having no trouble.

"Fine." She heard her own calm voice and wondered at the sound of it. But something in her *was* calm, because she was following him steadily. Her mind had gone still again in that peculiar, waiting way, and the roar of the ocean pounded at her senses with its throbbing rhythm.

She was dimly surprised when they reached the bottom and stepped out onto hard-packed sand. But she was not surprised that Mitch didn't release her hand. They began walking up the beach. The tide had been going out and was at the bottom of the ebb now, ready to turn. Within hours the strip of sand they walked on would be buried underneath churning water. Waves would crash against the base of the cliffs, sending spray to the top if the storm had arrived by then, and the sounds would be those of impotent fury.

"You were right about the stairs," Mitch said, looking at them as they walked past. "The support posts at the bottom look rotten, and the railing seems loose."

"Dangerous the way it is," she agreed. "I imagine stairs can't last very long when every high tide batters them. I'll probably have to replace them once a year." Had the realtor done that automatically? She made a mental note to call her lawyer and have him send her all the paperwork he had so she could see what had been done; the realtor's accounting to her had been the records only of the past year.

He glanced at her, then said, "So you're planning to live here from now on?"

"I'm thinking about it." The realization surprised her a little, because she knew it was true. She was considering the idea very seriously.

Mitch was silent for a few steps, then said, "It's a long way from Baltimore."

Kelly looked down at their clasped hands and then fixed her gaze ahead of them. His company was in Baltimore, the only roots he had left. Steadily, she said, "There are some places you just can't go back to. I'll never live in Baltimore again, Mitch. All I have there are graves."

His fingers tightened around hers almost convulsively, then relaxed. "I can't blame you for feeling that way. In fact, I was pretty sure you did. You've moved around a lot the past few years."

"Wanderlust," she said, making it casual.

"But now you're thinking of staying here?" His tone matched hers.

If I can. If he'll let me. "I like it here. And I love the house. It really threw me when I first saw it. My lawyer had been pestering me about appraisals and inventories, but I just didn't want to know the details. I suppose I still felt bitter toward your father. But I kept the place for some reason. The income took care of taxes and upkeep, so it didn't cost me anything. Until I was offered a job in the area, I was never tempted to come here."

That thought prompted another that had gotten lost in the first tense moments of meeting Mitch again, and she added slowly, "How did you know I was here?"

"The private investigator I hired found out once we traced you as far as Tucson."

"How?"

"Your next-door neighbors," Mitch replied. "A couple, apparently talkative."

Kelly stopped walking abruptly and turned to stare at him. "A couple?"

"An old couple." He frowned a little as he studied her expression. "Why? What's wrong?"

"Mitch . . . that building was for singles. There weren't any couples. And no one living there was over thirty-five." She was puzzled. More than that, really, although she couldn't define the feeling.

After a moment Mitch said slowly, "I didn't talk to them myself, but the investigator did. He said they were an old couple, and your next-door neighbors at the apartment building. That they were very friendly and talkative, and seemed to care about you. They told him you'd accepted a job with Cyrus Fortune's company in Portland."

"That doesn't make sense," she protested. "Nobody like that lived in the building; after six months I knew everyone at least by sight. Besides, I didn't tell anyone where I was going or whom I'd be working for."

"Maybe Fortune told them himself. As he was leaving your apartment?"

"If he was ever there, I didn't know about it. He came to my office at the company I was working for, ITC."

Mitch looked at her very intently, then said, "Why does it matter, Kelly?"

She realized she'd overreacted, that she shouldn't be so upset about this. Why would he have done it? What would be the point? But someone *had* sent her the newspaper clipping about Mitch. And someone had obviously told Mitch's investigator where she could be found. Something cold touched her spine.

"Kelly?"

Abruptly, she pulled her hand away from his, unable to bear the contact. A connection, the closing of a loop. What was the loop, she wondered. Time? A sequence of events she was caught up in and condemned to repeat endlessly? And, if so, what would take him away from her this time?

"Kelly, what the hell's wrong?" He reached out to grasp her shoulders. "Have you been hiding all these years? Running from something?"

With a wrenching effort she managed to drag all the scurrying fears back into their dark room and slam the door on them. Nerves, that's all, she told herself. That's all it was. The approaching storm was making her imagine things, making her tense and jumpy. And even if she wasn't, this time she couldn't run. That had already been decided.

She looked up at Mitch, her face composed again, eyes steady. Ignoring the last few questions, she said, "I just think it's odd, that's all. Just like I think it's odd your father left the house to me."

Mitch stared down at her for a moment, his mouth a grim slash. "Boyd told me he thought you were running, but I didn't want to believe him."

"Boyd?"

"My investigator."

In control again, she merely nodded. "Oh." She stepped back, shrugging off his hands, then glanced up at the leaden sky. "We'd better get back. The storm's almost here. And the tide's turned." The last observation, she thought, was strangely apt.

She began heading back toward the house. Without a word, but with no change in his dark expression, Mitch followed.

Evan Boyd let the binoculars fall to hang around his neck. He frowned as he stood in the concealing shadows of trees just outside the boundaries of the old Mitchell property. He'd been at this game too long to allow himself even a pang of guilt at observing others without their knowledge, but he had felt a bit uncomfortable watching the two on the beach. The emotional intensity between them was almost visible, so much so that he felt he'd intruded on a moment of extreme privacy.

He wasn't, officially, still working for John Mitchell. The morning his former employer had arrived in Portland and had heard the information about Kelly Russell, Boyd had received his final pay, a staggering bonus, and, despite Mitchell's obvious need to go to his lady immediately, sincere thanks.

It was what had kept Boyd in the area of Portland; having watched Mitchell put himself back together over the months, he had gotten rather more personally involved in this case than was usual for him, and he'd wanted to find out how it ended. And despite the fact that the job he'd been hired to do was done, he was still nagged by the feeling that something was wrong.

Now, having seen what had looked like the beginning of a confrontation on the beach that the lady had cut short, Boyd was sure of it. She was scared—and not of John Mitchell. She had the kind of command over herself that was born only from the deepest animal instincts of self-preservation.

He looked through the trees at the house just barely visible from his position. A big place; he'd nosed around and found out that a pretty good electronic security system protected the building itself, but the grounds were wide open and vulnerable. And he knew only too well that if somebody wanted to get inside the house, they could do it.

Assuming, of course, that the possibility of some kind of physical attack was what the lady was afraid of. And that was most likely; she didn't look the type to be shaken easily, so if someone was threatening her, she'd have to feel pretty damn sure the threats weren't empty ones.

The question was, who? Boyd had worked enough domestic cases to figure it was the ex-husband, but he was having trouble coming up with a motive. Kelly Russell had gotten an uncontested divorce and went back to using her maiden name. She hadn't accepted one dime in settlement or alimony, and there had been no children. Her ex was a wealthy man; Mitchell hadn't wanted to know, but Boyd had managed to find out a few facts about Bradford West and the man had no need to hound Kelly, not financially, anyway.

Still, Boyd's gut said it was West. And West, who owned a lucrative string of travel agencies, periodically turned managerial duties over to his second in command and disappeared for a few days or a week. Boyd didn't consider it a coincidence that on at least three past occasions the brief vacations closely matched the times when Kelly Russell had picked up and moved. It *had* to be West who was after her.

But why?

The private investigator brought the binoculars up to his eyes again and located Mitchell and his lady as they moved along one of the garden pathways to the house. Mitchell looked both strained and grim, and Kelly had the white, still face of a mask. Boyd whistled softly under his breath. Clamp a lid over too many emotions, and sooner or later there was going to be a hell of a bang. The two now going so quietly into the house had more than their fair share, and if they didn't let some of the pressure out soon, one or both of them would shatter into a million pieces.

He didn't want to watch that happen, but there was nothing he could do about it. The only thing he might possibly be able to do for them was to find out if West was around somewhere and bent on causing trouble. And if that was the case, Boyd had a few contacts in Portland as well as in other places. He just might be able to get something done.

A sudden gust of wind made him shiver and glance up at the heavy gray clouds that seemed to be leaning down on him. Pacific storms could be monsters, and this one rolling in looked as if it had at least a few fangs and claws.

He hated storms.

Kelly didn't mind storms. She hated to feel them approaching, but once they arrived she was fine. So when the wind began whistling and whining outside just minutes after they came into the house, she could feel some of her tension ease. But not all of it, because Mitch was too silent, too watchful; there was something in the stony set of his face that told her his breaking point was only a whisper away.

She could have retreated to her office, but didn't. She was trying to nerve herself to tell him the truth; if there was the slightest possibility he was in danger because he was near her, he had to know at least enough to be on his guard. And she had to admit the possibility.

When they came into the house, she went into the kitchen automatically. "This time I'll cook," she said without looking at him. "Is soup okay with you?"

"Fine." His voice was unnaturally soft.

Kelly kept her eyes on what she was doing as she reached into one of the cabinets for a pot, but said softly, "Take it easy, Mitch. I'm going to tell you. I just need a few minutes, all right?" She thought he needed the time more than she did, even though she still hadn't decided how much to tell him.

"All right," he said finally. "I'll go build up a fire in the den. We can talk better in there."

She listened as the wind wailed suddenly outside, and agreed. "Perfect weather for a fire." She didn't hear him go, but felt his absence. *We're both too wound up,* she acknowledged. Of course, it was barely twenty-four hours since he had reappeared in her life, and the entire situation was leaden with strangeness and too many emotions. It would have been impossible to resolve everything quickly even if they'd been able to try.

Kelly prepared the soup, half listening as the storm intensified outside and rain began pelting the windows. When the light meal was ready, she piled everything on a big tray, and Mitch appeared silently to carry it into the den. He had closed the drapes to shut out visible evidence of the storm's fury, and the room was softly lighted by lamps and the crackling fire.

She started to move toward one of the big chairs, then hesitated and chose instead to curl up at one corner of the couch, her shoes off, warming her cold hands on the soup mug. Mitch joined her there, a careful foot of space between them, and she wondered if he was as conscious of that distance as she was.

The question came a few minutes later, after they'd finished eating. "What are you running from, Kelly?"

"My ex-husband."

Mitch half nodded, as if he'd expected that response despite the way he'd phrased his question. "Why?"

Kelly looked down at the cup of coffee in her hand and thought that it all sounded so melodramatic. The police had made their opinion plain. "Because he wants to kill me."

Slowly, Mitch leaned forward to set his coffee cup on the table between them and the fireplace. Then he leaned back and half turned to look at her, waiting until she met his gaze. "He threatened to do that?"

She nodded, answering the next question before it could be asked. "And I believe him. He isn't one to make idle threats."

Mitch was frowning, looking more dangerous than she'd ever seen him, the firelight flickering over the black eye patch, his other eye narrowed. "Did you go to the police?"

Kelly laughed hollowly. "In three separate cities. But they can't arrest someone for threats, and I can't prove he would do anything more. My word against his, and he's very good at swaying people to believe him." She was still weighing in her mind how much to say, shying violently from the worst of it because she didn't think she could even say it aloud.

"Why does he want to hurt you?" Mitch didn't doubt what she was telling him, he was just finding it difficult to believe that anyone could look at Kelly's beautiful, delicate face, and think of violence.

"That's a more complicated answer." She looked away from him, turning her gaze to the fire. "Because I left him. It was a blow to his ego. Because I made him give me a divorce. He hates giving in to anyone, being forced to do something he doesn't want to do. But, most of all, because I know something about him that he doesn't want anyone else to know. He likes power, and I took some of his power away by holding a threat over his head."

"What threat?"

"I'd rather not talk about that, Mitch," she said carefully. "It isn't important. What's important is that the threat worked against him enough to get me my freedom, but nothing else. If I went public, it wouldn't stop him. He'd buy off somebody or find some other way out of the mess. Then he'd come after me."

"So you've been running." He watched her intently, saw how she almost flinched. Whatever she'd been at eighteen, Kelly was a strong woman now and she hated running; that, more than anything, told him how real the threat against her was.

"It seemed the only answer. At first I thought he'd get tired of the chase and quit, but not now. I settle into a new city, a new state, and sometimes months go by before I see him standing on a street corner watching me. Or pick up the phone and hear his voice. The first few times I called the police, and when they checked he was blamelessly in Marshall—his hometown in eastern Texas—and had witnesses to say he'd never left. Before I could pack up and move again, my apartment would be trashed, or my car vandalized."

"That didn't impress the police?"

Kelly leaned forward to set her cup on the coffee table, then shrugged as she sat back. "No. I was always living in large cities, and things like that happen. That's what they told me. I knew Brad had hired people to do his dirty work, but I couldn't prove it. After a while I stopped bothering with the police."

Brad. The name echoed in his mind, jabbing like a poisoned thorn. What kind of man was this Brad that he could terrorize a woman who had

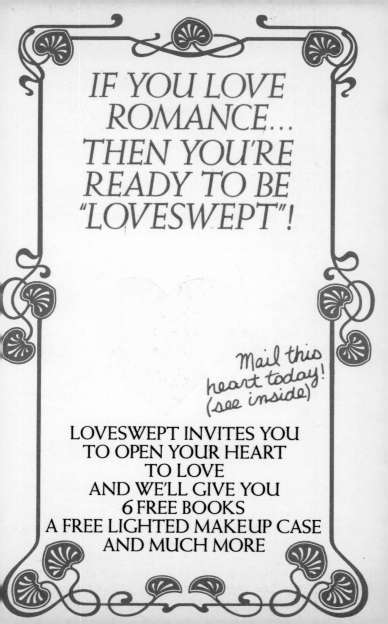

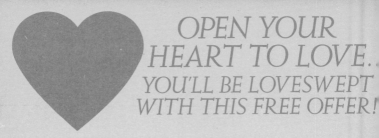

OPEN YOUR HEART TO LOVE...
YOU'LL BE LOVESWEPT WITH THIS FREE OFFER!

HERE'S WHAT YOU GET:

1. **FREE! SIX NEW LOVESWEPT NOVELS!** You get 6 beautiful stories filled with passion, romance, laughter, and tears...exciting romances to stir the excitement of falling in love... again and again.

2. **FREE! A BEAUTIFUL MAKEUP CASE WITH A MIRROR THAT LIGHTS UP!**
What could be more useful than a makeup case with a mirror that lights up*? Once you open the tortoise-shell finish case, you have a choice of brushes...for your lips, your eyes, and your blushing cheeks.

*(batteries not included)

3. **SAVE! MONEY-SAVING HOME DELIVERY!** Join the Loveswept at-home reader service and we'll send you 6 new novels each month. You always get 15 days to preview them before you decide. Each book is yours for only $2.09 — a savings of 41¢ per book.

4. **BEAT THE CROWDS!** You'll always receive your Loveswept books before they are available in bookstores. You'll be the first to thrill to these exciting new stories.

BE LOVESWEPT TODAY — JUST COMPLETE, DETACH AND MAIL YOUR FREE-OFFER CARD.

FREE – LIGHTED MAKEUP CASE!
FREE – 6 LOVESWEPT NOVELS!

- NO OBLIGATION
- NO PURCHASE NECESSARY

(DETACH AND MAIL CARD TODAY.)

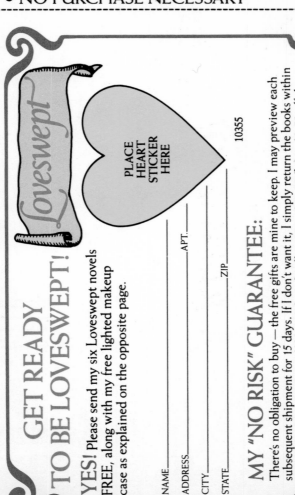

GET READY TO BE LOVESWEPT!

YES! Please send my six Loveswept novels FREE, along with my free lighted makeup case as explained on the opposite page.

PLACE HEART STICKER HERE

NAME _____

ADDRESS _____ APT. ____

CITY _____

STATE _____ ZIP _____

10355

MY "NO RISK" GUARANTEE:

There's no obligation to buy — the free gifts are mine to keep. I may preview each subsequent shipment for 15 days. If I don't want it, I simply return the books within 15 days and owe nothing. If I keep them I will pay just $12.50 (I save $2.50 off the retail price for 6 books) plus postage and handling and any applicable sales tax.

BRjfm

Prices subject to change. Orders subject to approval.

REMEMBER!

- The free books and gift are mine to keep!
- There is no obligation!
- I may preview each shipment for 15 days!
- I can cancel anytime!

(DETACH AND MAIL CARD TODAY.)

trusted him enough to marry him? And there was more, Mitch knew that. A knot of pain, a sickening rage grew inside him. Despite her even voice and expressionless face, he knew Kelly was deeply, coldly afraid of her ex-husband, and if she believed in the man's threats, it was simply because he had threatened before, and had acted on his threats.

"Kelly, what did he do to you?" Mitch heard his own harsh voice, and even though he wasn't sure he could bear hearing her answer, he knew that he had to hear it. He saw her flinch, saw her face go taut and her eyes widen as she stared blindly into the fire. Though she didn't move a muscle, he had the vivid impression that she had withdrawn into herself, as if some protective barrier had shattered at his blunt question and now she was trying frantically to hide herself away.

"Leave it alone, Mitch," she whispered.

"I can't." He leaned toward her, taking both her cold hands in his and feeling the tremor that wasn't visible. "And neither can you." He knew his voice was too harsh, but he couldn't do anything about it.

"I don't want to talk about it." Her voice was thready.

"Kelly, you have to." And he had to push this time, had to make her tell him. He didn't want to hear, God, no; just the thought of what must have been done to her made raw and murderous emotions knot inside him until he could hardly breathe. But it was all trapped inside her, memories he could only guess at, and until she let them out there could never be any healing.

"Please, I—"

"He beat you, didn't he?"

She flinched again, at his harsh voice or the bleakness of a small, hard word that meant pain and terror. Then, slowly, her wide eyes reflecting the leaping fires of a private hell, she nodded.

Mitch wanted to hold her, to wrap his arms around her tense, quivering body and take away her pain. But some new instinct told him that she wouldn't be able to tell him about this if he was too close, that if he touched more than her hands she'd break into thousands of pieces.

Somehow, he managed to cage his own emotions and soften the rasp of his voice. "Tell me, honey."

She shivered violently. "Don't. He called me that."

Mitch felt his teeth clamp together so hard that his jaw ached. The bastard. That he could have so defiled a simple endearment to make it unbearable to her. Holding her trembling hands gently but firmly, he repeated, "Tell me."

Still not looking at him, her voice soft and far-away, she murmured, "I used to see reports on television about women who were abused. And I would wonder how they could stay with men who hurt them. Then I found out. It's all too dreadfully easy. To believe the apologies and the promises. To look in the mirror and tell yourself the bruises and cuts will heal—because they have before. To be more afraid of being alone than of being hurt again."

"Kelly—"

She didn't seem to hear his low voice. "It wasn't so bad at first. He was very possessive, but he had a lot of charm and in those first weeks his demands were almost casual. Then one day he lost his temper and slapped me. I don't even remember what it was about. He was so sorry. Sent me flowers and a little gold bracelet. I thought he'd just lost control, and I wasn't afraid of him. Not then."

Mitch was silent, gazing at her white face and feeling so cold inside at the images her soft voice was painting for him. He had never in his life been so conscious of the implacable desire to choke the life out of another human being; if the bastard had been standing in front of him, Mitch would have watched him die and never felt a moment's regret.

Kelly was still staring at the fire, and her voice remained toneless. "The next time, he knocked me down. There were more apologies and flowers. I think I started to get scared then. He's a big man. Powerful. So I tried not to make him mad. I tried to be a good wife. But I was always doing something wrong. Saying the wrong thing, or—"

"Kelly, no. It wasn't your fault. You were the victim; you weren't to blame for what happened to you."

A faint frown disturbed the stillness of her face. "Wasn't I? I stayed with him. For almost a year. Even after I knew it wasn't going to stop. Even when it kept getting worse, I stayed with him. And I kept trying to be good. I'd see his face change, and I'd say I was sorry even though I didn't know what I'd done. He told me it was my fault, that I made him do it, and I believed him. And when he—the two times he had to take me to a doctor, I said what he told me to, that I'd fallen downstairs. The doctor knew, but Brad paid him a lot of money and I realized he wouldn't report it."

God, how badly she must have been hurt for that son of a bitch to take her to a doctor! Mitch was holding himself still with iron will, but he could feel his own muscles jerking in a blind response to his pain and fury.

"The doctor kept his records, though. I bought them from him later. That was what I used to make Brad give me a divorce, the medical records. I hired a lawyer, and he threatened to make it all public. Brad couldn't stand that."

Mitch swallowed his own rage. "What finally made you leave him?" he asked, not sure he wanted to hear the answer.

"I didn't realize what was happening to me for a long time," she murmured. "But then, one day, he came home and just started in on me for no reason at all. And I found myself . . . cowering . . . against the wall, in a corner. Like a terrified animal."

She turned her head and looked at him for the first time, her beautiful, wounded eyes stark with the memory of that moment. "An animal. That's what he'd turned me into. And I knew that being alone was better than being that."

Five

Swearing so softly that his voice was barely audible, Mitch gathered her stiff body into his arms and held her on his lap. She didn't resist, but she didn't respond at all to his gentleness. When he drew her head down to his shoulder, she allowed it to remain there, but her fingers were linked together tensely on her thighs.

He could feel her shivering, like something drawn too tight and about to snap. He wrapped both arms around her, unconsciously rocking a little, resting his cheek against her soft hair. When he could finally stop the silent oaths rising up from deep inside him where rage coiled tightly, he murmured in a husky voice, "It wasn't your fault," because he felt that she thought it somehow was her fault. "You didn't do anything—*not anything* —to deserve that, sweetheart."

"Yes, I did." Her voice was very quiet. "I left you."

It jolted him, even more because of his own unreasonable feelings of bitterness and betrayal.

For the first time, he felt those corrosive emotions releasing their hold on him; after what Kelly had suffered, both jealousy and bitterness seemed petty indeed.

"Listen to me." His voice was as quiet as hers had been. "You can't go on feeling guilty about that. We can't have it between us. Kelly, I've seen my medical records and I know what the doctors told you. When I woke up, almost the first words out of a doctor's mouth were that nobody had expected me to recover. You had every reason to believe them, and no reason at all to go on waiting for me."

"But here you are," she murmured. "I should have known you'd make it, no matter what anyone said. I should have loved you enough to believe that."

His arms tightened around her. "None of us can see the future, and fate tricks all of us. It wasn't a question of loving enough, that wouldn't have changed anything. You didn't leave me; *I* left *you*. God knows it wasn't my choice, but it happened. And you lost everyone else as well. Kelly, I wish we could both go back and start over, but we can't. You said it yourself; we have to go forward. You have to accept the fact that you have nothing to feel guilty about. And the fact that you could never have done anything bad enough to deserve what that bastard did to you."

The stiffness was seeping out of her slender body slowly, and her voice was less deadened when she spoke. "My head knows that, but the feelings . . . I've asked myself a thousand times how I could have stayed with him. I was afraid of being alone but, even deeper than that, I think some part of me really did feel that I deserved to be hurt."

"You didn't. You don't."

She stirred on his lap, and he loosened his hold enough for her to sit up. She looked at him steadily, something hesitant in her eyes, then said, "The guilt was . . . complicated. I felt guilty for leaving you and, at the same time, guilty because I couldn't really let you go."

He lifted one hand and cupped her cheek gently. He could feel his heart thudding in sudden hope, feel the satiny softness of her skin beneath his touch as his thumb brushed her cheekbone slowly. "You said you buried me," he reminded her.

Her eyes skittered away, then returned to his face. "That wasn't exactly true. I thought it was. The—the last time I went to see you, I even said good-bye to you, out loud. I knew I wasn't coming back. And I was very calm then. I must have driven about a hundred miles before I had to stop the car because I couldn't see the road."

Mitch started to draw her toward him, his hand slipping to the nape of her neck, but stopped when she shook her head slightly in a tiny protest. Her eyes were still fixed on his face. In the same soft, hesitant voice, she went on.

"I thought it was over. Then, a few months later, I met Brad. You asked if I loved him. That was one of the reasons I felt guilty, because I couldn't. I could never say it to him, even later when I'd say anything else he wanted to hear. I'd told him about you, and once—once when he was angry he said that there was a ghost in his bed. That I couldn't love him the way I should have because of you. And I realized I hadn't said good-bye to you at all, I'd just walked away."

He drew a short breath, then said, "Why did you lie to me?"

Kelly's shoulders lifted slightly and then relaxed. "What else could I have said? Mitch, I knew the girl you had loved was gone. And I'd learned that I couldn't take being possessed. Everything had changed."

"And now?" he asked quietly.

She gave that confused little shrug again. "Now? I don't know. It seemed so simple yesterday. You needed an ending and I did too. I thought we only had to spend a little time together to find that ending. But you'd changed in ways I hadn't expected. You aren't the man I remember, the man I couldn't let go of, and yet I feel a—a connection to you."

"I know."

"How can you?"

"Because I feel it too." Holding her diffident gaze with his own, he said slowly, "And it's more than it ever was ten years ago, Kelly. It's strong, and painful, and complicated, and it scares the hell out of me."

"It does?"

He sighed roughly. "Of course it does. We're both totally different people, almost strangers, but not quite. Ten years ago you were Kelly. Just Kelly. God forgive me, I didn't *think* about you. I felt about you, but I didn't think. And when I looked at you, I saw copper hair and violet eyes and a smile. Nice and simple."

"But now it isn't."

Mitch laughed, a low sound. "No. No, now it isn't. I think about you all the time. Copper hair and violet eyes. But now the eyes are shadowed and the hair's more golden than I remember. I see strength and hurt and intelligence. I see a woman instead of a girl. But not a stranger. My mind tells me it'll take years to know you the way I need to, but my heart knows you now. And the one thing I'm certain of most of all is that I can't hold on to you. As badly as I want to, I know I'll lose you for good if I do."

Kelly looked at him, so close, so different from the man he had been. She had stopped deceiving herself into believing that she wanted an ending between them, but she was afraid of being that vulnerable again. She knew without a shadow of a doubt that Mitch would never hurt her physically, but there were so many other ways of being hurt, intentionally or not. And no guarantees. He might not be able to conquer his own possessive nature; she might well discover that her own ability to love completely had been destroyed by Brad's cruelty; they could find there was just too much between them, too many memories, too many changes.

She started to move from his lap, but his arms tightened gently around her.

"Kelly, I know you're scared. I know neither of us is the person we were ten years ago. But the changes have made us both stronger, and there are ties between us that haven't been broken. We both feel that."

She half nodded. "I know. I'm just not sure what it means. I don't know what I feel. And I've made so many mistakes. I don't think I could bear to make another one." This time he released her so that she could stand.

Mitch sat looking up at her, forcing himself to remain still because he could sense her need for distance. "I think it's worth the risk," he said quietly. "I don't believe we could ever be a mistake, Kelly. But I want you to understand something. Whatever we find together can't be built on guilt. You have to come to me because you want to—not because you feel you owe me."

She hesitated, then said, "Yesterday you said that I did owe you."

"I'm sorry for that," he responded instantly. His firm lips twisted slightly. "I didn't want you to throw me out without giving us a chance, but I should never have said that. The only thing we owe to each other is honesty. I left you without being given a choice; you walked away from me because nobody could give you any hope at all that I'd come out of the coma."

"And you don't blame me for that?" She had taken a couple of steps away, toward the fireplace, and didn't look at him as she asked the difficult question.

Mitch hesitated, but his own determination that they be honest with each other compelled him to be truthful about it. "Blame isn't the right word. There's a part of me—an unthinking, unreasoning part—that feels bitter. Maybe even betrayed. But it's fading away, I promise you."

"What if it doesn't?" She looked at him through eyes that felt hot and painfully dry. "What if you can never completely forgive me for not waiting?"

He rose to his feet, but didn't attempt to get closer to her. Very slowly, he said, "Kelly, if you *had* waited, if I'd awakened to find you beside my bed, I think we would have lost something very special, something we're only now finding."

"Why?"

"Because in most ways you'd still be that girl I loved but never really thought about. Waiting for anything is a kind of limbo; you wouldn't have changed very much if you had waited all those years for me. You're different today not because of Keith's death or your parents' but because you learned a very hard lesson about being alone. And the first step in learning what you had to was walking away from me. If you hadn't learned that lesson, if I'd awakened to find you there waiting, I would have held on even tighter to a woman I'd never tried to understand. And I think you would have been lost to me."

Kelly understood what he meant. They would have been tied together by the past, yet neither would have been forced to find the self-awareness required to see each other as distinct and separate individuals. Like two strangers holding hands in the darkness, their tie would have been one of fear and loneliness. Better to be together than alone.

She met his steady gaze and swallowed hard. "I have to hear it, Mitch. I have to know you mean it."

He nodded, a muscle flexing in his hard jaw. "And you have to believe that even the unreasoning part of me means it, don't you?"

"Yes. Maybe it isn't rational, but I can't let go of the guilt until I know you forgive me."

"All right." His smile was a little strained. "I'll work on it."

Reprieve. The word rose in Kelly's mind. Once again they had only briefly obeyed the pull drawing them together, coming near enough to each other to confront one of the barriers between them. Near enough, this time, to touch fleetingly. Then, cautiously, easing back again to a safe distance, gazing warily at each other across the space between them.

She resisted an impulse to give in completely to

the constant tug toward Mitch, just to allow herself to rush across the space and be in his arms. Even though it was where she wanted to be, every instinct told her that if she gave in too easily and without thought, she'd never learn to understand and value what she could have with him. And without understanding and respect, even love could turn into a trap all too easily.

Love? Love . . .

She drew a deep breath and flexed her shoulders in an attempt to ease the sudden tension. No, she realized, not sudden; it was just that the pull toward him had intensified so sharply, it felt like an entirely new thing. She hadn't dared define her own feelings until now, and giving them a name had weakened her resistance to him.

"I think I'd better go back to work for a while," she said carefully.

Mitch seemed to hesitate, then said, "Out on the beach, you were upset. Do you think your—do you think he's found you here? Is that what was bothering you?"

He found it very difficult to name Brad as her ex-husband, she realized. She wondered if he'd ever be able to accept the fact that she had married another man. The old Mitch wouldn't have been able to, she knew.

"I don't know," she said finally. "He had a private detective following me at one time; I thought I'd lost him before Tucson. But maybe I never did. Brad could be around here somewhere. He could be back in Texas. Just be careful, all right? He's dangerous."

Mitch nodded slowly, watching her.

She started toward the door, feeling as if the dying storm outside had battered her mercilessly.

"Kelly?"

Pausing at the door, she looked back at him. He was grave, his lean face still.

"Happy Valentine's Day," he said softly.

Whatever slim resistance she had left almost deserted her then. Whether it would have been best if the accident had never happened, or if she had waited, or even if their best chance for happiness was right now, the fact remained that they would have been married ten years ago today.

Unable to say a word, Kelly simply nodded and hurried from the room. She went to her study and closed the door firmly behind her, leaning back against it for a moment. Then she walked to her desk and sat down, staring blindly at the neat stacks of files and charts and graphs.

She loved Mitch. For the second time in her life, she had fallen in love with him. Or maybe she had never stopped in the first place; maybe that emotion had grown and changed silently inside her all these years. It had changed, she knew that. This wasn't the unshadowed adoration of a child, it was the painful, uncertain love of a woman. This time she was afraid of love. *Could* she love him the way a man needed to be loved? Could she give so much of herself without becoming lost?

And what about Mitch? Even assuming he could truly forgive her for not having waited, for marrying another man, could he love the woman she was now? Could he conquer his own possessiveness, trust her enough to give her the space she needed? And once they were lovers . . .

Lovers. Kelly shivered, wondering if Mitch had guessed the part of it she'd been unable to say. Sex hadn't been something she had enjoyed with Brad. Quite the contrary, in fact. He hadn't been brutal—except in the weeks just before she'd left—but always he'd been impatient and rough. The first time had been terrible, the last time even worse. More than once, he had used sex as a punishment because he'd known how she hated it, and though she understood that his way had been twisted and sick, she couldn't help but wonder if he had left her physically and emotionally unable to enjoy it.

She knew that what she felt for Mitch was made up of desire as well as love, but she was still afraid that if he made love to her, she'd be unable to respond. She might feel what she had with Brad: the smothered helplessness of being pinned by a male body and used.

Brad had seen it on her face, had felt it in her tense body no matter how hard she'd tried to hide it; that had been one of the sparks igniting his rages. She wasn't sure even now if he had been hurt by it or if his tremendous ego had simply demanded that every woman consider him a wonderful lover. Whichever it had been, he had blamed her for her failure to find pleasure in his bed. Her and the ghost of Mitch he had seen between them. And his anger had found expression in taunts and cold humiliations and painful demands.

It had been years, but she hadn't forgotten.

What if those memories proved to be yet another barrier between her and Mitch?

After a long time Kelly made herself lift the first of the files from the neat stack in front of her on the desk. She'd had a lot of practice in blanking her mind, and she called on that now. With careful focus she concentrated on the work.

• • •

Mitch remained in the den for a long time after Kelly had gone, looking at nothing. Finally, he got the tray from the coffee table and carried it into the kitchen. He efficiently cleared away the remains of their lunch, his brooding glance straying often to the wall phone hanging near the pantry. There were two separate phone lines into the house: one ending in the study and the other in the kitchen; the kitchen phone had an extension in the entrance hall.

It took Mitch only a few minutes to make up his mind. He went to the phone and punched a number that was very familiar since he'd called it often in the past year. This time, however, the only response was an answering machine with a terse request to leave a name and number. Mitch hung up without leaving a message, and stood thinking for a moment.

His second call, this one to a hotel in Portland, met with more success. He asked for Evan Boyd, and was immediately given a mobile phone number where he could be reached.

Mitch wasn't very surprised to find that Boyd was still in the area. He called the mobile phone, and when the investigator answered, said only, "Mitchell. Where are you?"

There was a brief pause, and then Boyd replied somewhat defensively, "Just down the road. I know you gave me my walking papers, but—"

"Something was bothering you?"

"Yeah. Something."

Hearing the constraint in the other man's voice, Mitch sighed and said, "All right. I admit I didn't want to hear that Kelly was running from someone. But you were right."

"Her ex?" Boyd asked cautiously.

"The bastard's threatened to kill her. Have you been watching the house?"

"Off and on. I haven't seen a sign of anyone else, but I've been around mostly during the day."

Mitch wondered briefly if Kelly would like this, but the question didn't alter his determination. He could no more ignore a threat against her than he could willfully prevent the next beat of his heart. Slowly, he said, "Can you find out if he's where he's supposed to be . . . in Texas?"

Boyd cleared his throat. "Already done. I called his travel agency in Marshall and talked to his secretary. He's supposedly been on vacation, out of the country. But my gut says he's a hell of a lot closer than that."

Mitch almost smiled—at the informant rather than the information. "All right, then. Since you've obviously been working for me all along, forget the walking papers. I want that bastard out of Kelly's life for good. What are our options?"

"We don't have many, until he makes a move. I know a few cops out here, but whether they'll be able to do anything is something I can't say until I talk to them."

"Do that right away. And make them understand it's serious. Kelly doesn't scare easily, and she's sure he really means to kill her. From what she's told me, I think he's capable of it. He's hurt her before." It was difficult for Mitch even to get the words out, and his tone harshened when it managed it.

In a flattened voice Boyd said, "I wondered. Couldn't find a sane motive for him to have gone after her. Look, do I have your approval to hire a couple more men to watch the house? We'll concentrate on a perimeter defense—the road and the beach—and stay well back from the house. I can promise you that the men I pick will be invisible."

"Hire as many as you think necessary."

"Okay. I should have them on the job by tonight. And I'll talk to the cops."

They spoke only a few moments longer, setting a time for Mitch to call the following day to check on the progress that had been made. Then the call ended, and Mitch stood looking around the kitchen without really seeing it.

Brad. Almost as much as ending the threat to Kelly, Mitch wanted to get his hands on that bastard. It wouldn't take long, he thought with the detachment that came from a soul-deep, icy rage. Not long at all. Just long enough to teach *him* what real fear was. Just long enough to break every bone in his body.

The next two days passed quietly. Mitch had said that waiting for anything was a kind of limbo, and Kelly felt he was right. It was as if they were both waiting for something definitive. Between them was a careful stillness, like the quiet before a storm. They talked during meals, but nothing important was said. She buried herself in her work for long hours at a stretch, and except for making certain she ate, Mitch didn't try to interfere with her schedule.

The cleaning service came to do the house, and gardeners came to spend a day working on the grounds, and Kelly had another dream with a chilling ending.

It was the second night after she'd told Mitch about her marriage. She woke near dawn, a scream trapped in her throat. She was sitting up in bed, shaking, the terrifying images of the dream vivid in her mind. This time she'd found Mitch in the lower garden, and everything had been fine at first. But then he had kissed her, his touch tender, and she had felt only coldness and dread. His puzzled hurt had turned with nightmare swiftness to anger, to a driven determination to *make* her feel something else. His face changed so horribly that she had become afraid of him. He had pulled her down into a tangle of ivy, his bitter voice like knives.

"Now his ghost is between us, damn you!"

She had watched his savage face over her, blotting out the light—and woke with that scream in her throat.

It was hours until dawn, but Kelly wasn't ready to go back to sleep. She slid from the bed and, without bothering to turn on a light, went to her door and opened it silently. As soon as she stepped out into the hall, she saw the faint glow of a light underneath Mitch's door. Was he still up? For the first time, she wondered if he had trouble sleeping now. She thought that if she had awakened to find nine years of her life gone, sleep would be something to fear, something she would need to hold at bay.

It wasn't enough that fate had stolen time from him, but to further deny him the necessary peace of sleep and dreams . . . just the thought of it filled her with pain for him.

For an instant she was tempted to knock on his door and ask if she could help, but she resisted the urge because her dream was still too fresh in her mind. And because . . . She glanced down at her sheer white nightgown, telling herself that it was hardly something to wear while paying a post-midnight visit to a man one had been trying to keep at a distance.

On bare feet she slipped silently past his door and continued down the hall. She went downstairs, the house looking oddly unfamiliar, the way houses always seemed to in the darkest part of the night. The central heating was working well; even with her scanty attire and bare feet she didn't feel at all cold. She had come down here without thought, and ended up in the conservatory. Moonlight was shining into the room, and there was something welcoming about the wicker furniture glowing palely in the center of dark, glossy plants.

She curled up on the blue and yellow cushions of the chaise, looking out at the rain-washed flagstones of the terrace without really seeing them. This was the warmest room in the house, the temperature and humidity carefully controlled because of the plants, and despite her thin nightgown she felt comfortable. In fact, within minutes she was aware of heavy eyelids and an almost irresistible urge to sink down into the cushions and recapture sleep. Common sense told her she should go back upstairs to bed, but she couldn't find the will to move.

Without noticing the transition, she fell asleep.

A ghost? No. A touch, light as a feather, warm on her lips. A sharp, clean scent like spices and rain. A sense of closeness, a connection made. She could feel herself floating upward through white mist, drawn from sleep by something she had no power, no will to resist. Something inevitable. Inside her, the waiting stillness gave way to yearning, reaching, needing. She was afraid to open her eyes. More afraid not to.

Mitch was bent over her, sitting on the edge of the chaise as he looked down at her. His hard face was softened, his eye so dark it seemed bottomless. An inexpressibly tender smile was on his firm lips.

Kelly realized vaguely that it was early morning, that light filled the conservatory, and that he had kissed her.

"Good morning," he said softly.

She couldn't look away from his compelling gaze, feeling a quivering uncertainty deep inside herself. "Good morning. I—I didn't mean to fall asleep down here." Her voice was as quiet as his had been.

"You were smiling," he said. "I should have let you sleep; you looked so peaceful."

She didn't feel peaceful now. The emotions that had followed her out of sleep were growing stronger, and he was too close for her to fight them. Had he kissed her, or had that been only a wistful part of her dream? She wanted him to kiss her. She had to know how it would make her feel, had to know if love would make a difference.

Desire must have shown on her face or in her eyes, because it was clear he saw it. A muscle tightened suddenly in his jaw, and his voice dropped to a low, husky note. "Don't look at me like that."

"Like what?" She was hardly aware that her own voice was unsteady. Without thought, and for the first time, she touched him, her hand lifting to his lean cheek. She could feel a muscle flex under her fingers, feel how smoothly and tautly his tanned skin fit over his bones.

Mitch caught his breath and went briefly still as her soft hand touched his face, then his own hand lifted and held hers against him. "Kelly, I want you so much, I'm half out of my mind with it. I've wanted you since you were fourteen years old." His voice was rougher now, strained. "I can't be casual about it. Once I start loving you, I might not be able to stop. I'm not even sure I have any control left."

He wondered if she realized just how literally he meant what he'd just said. Whatever the strength and motivations of his love for Kelly ten years earlier, his desire had been strong and focused totally on her. He had waited with what patience he could muster for her to leave childhood behind, to become the woman he needed. And then, nine long years of nothing, not even dreams he could remember, and more than another year of intense therapy to repair the ravages of the coma.

Now he was in better physical shape than ever before in his life. He had begun coping with most of his losses, had even accepted the knowledge that neither he nor Kelly were the people they had been. Emotionally, he was still struggling to come to terms with the changes.

But his desire for her, restrained for so long by patience and fate and circumstance, had changed only in growing stronger and more complex. He wanted her so badly that he was half afraid the depth of his need would frighten her.

She was looking up at him, her beautiful violet eyes darkened almost to purple, and he could see desire there as well as a faint uncertainty. She didn't draw her hand away. "Is that another warning?" she asked softly.

He hesitated. "I don't want to ruin things between us by rushing this. If you aren't sure, don't start something you might not be able to stop."

Kelly didn't have to debate her response to that. She knew, maybe she had always known, that this, at least, had to be resolved. They had never been lovers, and if they were to build any kind of future together, they would have to find out if they could be. And there was only one way to discover that answer. She was aware of a small, nervous anxiety deep inside her about her own ability to respond to him, but stronger than that was the unfamiliar yearning that wouldn't let go of her.

She wanted him. Her body wanted his with a craving that had built inside her for years.

"I'm not sure of anything," she said at last. "Except that I've always regretted we were never lovers. Whatever happens this time, I don't want to regret it again."

"You were so young then," he murmured, his free hand lifting to cup her cheek. "And you didn't feel what I felt."

She was surprised. "You knew that?"

"I knew. You were like a flower opening up, shy and a little bit afraid." His mouth tightened suddenly. "I wish—"

Kelly didn't have to hear the rest of the broken-off sentence to know what it was he wished. She wished it too. She wished that he had been her first lover. But, in a very real sense, she thought he would be. Brad had been the first man in her bed, but he hadn't been a lover.

"Mitch—"

"Never mind," he said huskily, leaning down until his lips were a whisper away from hers. He had to believe he could conquer his jealousy, and he wasn't about to let those dark feelings become a barrier between them. "You're with me now, and that's all that matters."

She tensed almost instinctively at his first touch, but the instant surge of sensations and emotions was so overpowering that she forgot to be nervous. His mouth was warm and hard, the hunger in him stark and unhidden, and everything inside her responded with a blind need that held no room for memories. Her arms went up around his neck and her mouth opened for the shockingly intimate, incredibly arousing thrust of his tongue. Desire washed over her in a hot wave.

She hadn't known. Even the long-ago shy excitement that Mitch's desire had roused in her hadn't prepared her for the taut pleasure his touch brought. Her entire body came fully alive for the first time, as if she'd been sleepwalking all her life, her senses muffled or blunted behind some gauzy curtain she hadn't known was there. Her very nerve endings reacted as though to an electrical shock, blasting impulses of fiery sensation from her head to her toes.

Both his arms were around her, lifting her up from the cushions so that she was held tightly against him. The hardness of his chest pressed her breasts, and she felt them ache with a sudden throb that made her shudder helplessly. The intensity was so unexpected and unfamiliar, it was like a blow that scattered all rational thoughts, and she was aware of astonished wonder that it was possible to feel this way.

She hadn't known.

He kissed her as if the ten long years between them could be banished by this simple act, as if the sheer force of his own longing could change time itself. And, in a sense, it did and could do just that. Kelly lost all awareness of time and place, all perception of herself as different from the girl Mitch had once loved. None of that mattered. There was only right now, only these incredible feelings.

"Kelly . . ." He lifted his head at last, staring down at her with a gaze like black fire. She could only look up at him in wonder, everything that was female in her responding wildly to the need written so vividly on his face. The very bones beneath his bronze skin seemed sharpened, drawing the flesh tight, the planes and angles of his lean face more distinct, curiously more primitive and profoundly male than ever before. The black slash of the eye patch was, for the first time, an inherent part of him.

Pirates. Rakes and heartbreakers.

Thickly, his voice so rough and strained it was barely audible, he said, "If you want me to stop . . . tell me now . . . while I still can."

The desire for him that was pulsing through Kelly's body with every beat of her heart was more real than uncertainty or anxiety could ever be, and her response was as unthinking as her next breath. Her arms tightened around his neck, and she pressed closer to him. "Don't stop," she whispered.

A rough sound like a growl emanated from his throat as he bent his head and kissed her again, deeply. Then he slipped one arm beneath her knees and rose, holding her with an easy strength that made her catch her breath. She clung to him as he carried her through the house to the stairs, her eyes fixed on his face.

Six

Mitch carried her to the master bedroom, where the bed she had abandoned in the middle of the night was just as she had left it, the covers tumbled and pushed back. He bent and placed her in the middle of the wide bed and then joined her, his hard body pressed close to her side as he propped himself on an elbow and kissed her deeply.

Her senses were spinning and her body seemed filled with liquid fire, but when his mouth trailed downward to the lacy neckline of her nightgown she was again conscious of the small, cold lump of anxiety inside her. What if she couldn't respond to him?

"Mitch? I've never . . . I don't know if I can—" She broke off, not knowing how to explain. Even though she trusted him and wanted no shadow of Brad's cruelty to mar this for either of them, she had to bite back an urge to beg him not to hurt her.

It was so bright in the room, leaving her nowhere to hide, prompting unwanted memories of

Brad's impatience at her shyness and modesty. She didn't want to remember, but couldn't help herself; the way he had taunted her and forced her to strip in full light under his narrowed, probing gaze had disturbed her deeply, especially since he had been prone to make disparaging remarks about her body.

Kelly closed her eyes tightly as she tried to push the memories away. They were a cruel intrusion, an inescapable reminder of the scars Brad had left her with, and she could feel the lump of anxiety inside her growing larger as she struggled to overcome it.

"Look at me, sweetheart," Mitch murmured.

She opened her eyes slowly, seeing his face still stamped with that primitive male intensity, and yet the hard expression was tempered by the tender, sensual curve of his lips. The cold memories began to recede as the sheer presence of him filled her mind.

In a soft, rough voice, he said, "You know I could never hurt you." It wasn't a question—but it was.

After a moment the arms that had remained stiffly at her sides lifted to curve around his neck. "I know that," she whispered. "But there were so many dreams for so long, and reality can never measure up. I'm just afraid that . . . that I won't please you."

He brushed a strand of coppery hair away from her cheek, and his voice dropped to a tauter, less controlled note. "It isn't just that, is it? It's him. His ghost between us. What he did to you, the fear he made you feel."

Like her dream, but different. He wasn't angry, not in the way that had frightened her dream self.

But this was hurting him, and not just on that unreasoning level of himself where jealousy and a sense of betrayal lurked. "Mitch—"

"I can stand knowing he was a part of your life. I can even stand knowing he was the first man in your bed. But I can't stand having him between us, Kelly."

The intrusion. She could almost hear Brad laughing in satisfaction, and the cold echoes of that made a sudden new anger rise inside her. "I don't want him here," she said in a shaking voice. "But there was no one to drive him away, don't you understand? He isn't between *us*—he's just here, inside me, cold and ugly."

Mitch's arm tightened across her waist, and for an instant his face looked even more primitive. Then the drawn expression eased, and he leaned down to kiss her. His lips moved over hers, warm, slowly hardening as desire built, and she barely heard him mutter against her mouth, "I'll be inside you."

Not a threat, but a vow, she thought dimly as heat washed over her in waves. Consciously, she closed her mind to memories and hurts and fears, feeling her senses open up again in that unfamiliar, dizzying way. Her fingers twined in his thick dark hair, her mouth responding to his hunger with an increasing fervor of her own. The slow waves of heat were changing, hotter now and faster, flooding through her body with a force that left no room for anything else.

Kelly caught her breath as his lips left hers to trail down her neck. She kept her eyes closed, only distantly aware of the soft little sounds purring in the back of her throat. His mouth left fire wherever it touched, and a strange, coiling tension was born inside her, gripping her body like nothing she'd ever felt before. It was becoming difficult to breathe, and her breasts ached intolerably, and she wanted badly to *move,* to twist and press herself closer to him because she had to, because it was what her body and senses craved.

She felt his mouth move down over her breastbone, over the lacy neckline of her gown, and then felt the moist heat of his touch through the sheer cotton. One of his hands slid over her rib cage and surrounded a breast, his long fingers kneading her swollen flesh gently just as his mouth found the other nipple and closed over it. She jerked as pleasure shuddered through her entire body. His mouth on her, even through the material of the gown, sent jolts of exquisite sensation along every quivering nerve.

Mitch made a rough sound deep in his throat, and reached to pull the hem of her nightgown up. She lifted her hips instinctively as the material caught under her, then felt his strong arm beneath her back as he raised her slightly. The gown was pulled up over her head, and as soon as her arms were free of the sleeves she curved them around his neck again. Only then did her eyes drift open.

Another kind of heat rose in her cheeks as she realized that she was naked—and he was still fully clothed. But before she could give in to embarrassment, she saw the way he was looking at her, and her distress vanished. If she had felt each glance from him before, it was nothing compared to this. For the first time in her life, she was totally aware of her woman's body and all the uses nature had intended it for. Hunger burned in his gaze so intensely that she felt the stark heat of it touch her. She was hardly aware of not breathing as she stared up at the taut, absorbed expression on his face.

He was on her left so that she was looking at the right side of his face, and the thin black strap of his eye patch angling over his forehead above his eyebrow looked somehow more noticeable than the patch itself. She thought fleetingly about his offhand comment that he'd assumed the eye patch roused the maternal instinct in women, and knew that her own assessment had been far more accurate. There was nothing in him of a bird with a broken wing; he gave off too much intensity for any woman to look at him that way.

Pirates, rakes, and heartbreakers.

For the first time she couldn't help but wonder if Mitch had been with another woman since he'd awakened. Or even during the years before the accident. How complacent teenagers were, she reflected. It had not occurred to her then that a healthy man at the peak of his sexuality was hardly likely to wait idly for his virgin bride to mature. Then his rough voice drove the thought from her mind.

"Kelly . . . Lord, you're so beautiful . . ." He bent over her again, his face nuzzling between her breasts, and she gasped as the hovering tension began drawing tightly inside her again. Instinctively, needing to be close to him, her fingers fumbled at the buttons of his shirt. He helped her, stripping off the shirt and tossing it aside, but made no effort to remove the rest of his clothes. Instead, he concentrated wholly on her. His hands and lips caressed her breasts as if the very texture of her flesh utterly fascinated him.

He watched intently as his stroking thumbs

made her nipples stiffen and darken, then teased the hard points with the tip of his tongue and gently nibbling lips. Resisting the pressure of her arms as she tried to draw him closer, he continued the maddening caresses until a moan of tormented ecstasy emerged from her straining throat. Then his mouth clamped down hard over her nipple, his tongue stroking roughly, and Kelly writhed helplessly as wildfire raced through her.

Her mind whirling and senses shattering, Kelly couldn't believe it was possible to feel these things. Her body was being tossed about by waves of pleasure so intense it was almost painful. Was painful. Tension pulled her quivering muscles taut, and there was an aching emptiness inside her that swelled moment by moment until it threatened to consume her. She dimly heard sounds— soft, wild sounds—and knew they were coming from her.

She felt his hand moving slowly down over her belly, then lower, and her legs parted of their own volition. His touch was starkly intimate, a gentle probing that found her wet, swollen flesh and then stroked lazily. Kelly gritted her teeth unconsciously as her body arched in an unthinking response, and the soft sounds welling up and escaping became desperate. His mouth was on her breasts, his fingers moving over her throbbing flesh with a mysterious, stunning rhythm that her body reacted to with a violence of sensation.

Some part of her mind not swamped by the quickening surges of pleasure reflected with an uncaring idleness that she was going to die from this. It wasn't possible, she thought, to feel this intensely and not die. Her nerve endings were raw and her body was quivering on the edge of something that had to be death because nothing else could possibly be so shattering . . . and she didn't care if it killed her. Then there was an instant that was too powerful, her entire body shrieking in a taut silence, and a wild cry tore from her throat as she went over the edge. But it wasn't death, it was burning, throbbing ecstasy that exploded inside her with a force that seemed to melt her. For an eternal moment she was liquid, formless, pulsing.

Kelly was hardly aware when he gently unlocked her arms from around his neck and rolled off the bed. Limp and totally unable to move, she gradually came back to herself and to the realization that he was rapidly undressing. She forced her eyes to open, somehow startled by the brightness of the room, and looked at him as the last of his clothing was thrown aside.

He wanted her, the swollen fullness of his loins a mute testament to raging desire. And, once more but only for an instant, that primitive male hunger almost frightened her. The black fire of his gaze, the hard, powerful body filled with a strength she could never fight if he chose to turn it against her. And yet . . . he was beautiful like this. Beautiful and deeply moving in a way she'd never thought a man could be, as primitive and compelling as any wild creature but tugging painfully at her heart and senses because he was a man.

Until now the only experience Kelly had had of male sexuality was impatience and the seemingly driven compulsion to find release in a female body. She hadn't understood how desire could be emotional as well, so all-consuming, and since she had never felt it herself during her marriage, any sign of Brad's arousal had made her nervous and wary. Because, once aroused, he had been intent only on satisfying the demands of his body.

Now, as Mitch went still for an instant as he stood by the bed, she looked at him and felt the coiling, heated tension rising inside her again. And she felt no fear or wariness of him or of his desire. He had taught her to feel pleasure in the response of her own body to desire, and her cold anxiety had melted away in the heat of that fire.

Half consciously, she held out her arms to him, and Mitch made a low, rough sound as he rejoined her on the bed. His fingertip-hold on control was rapidly deserting him; he hadn't dared undress before now because he'd known that his pounding need for her would overwhelm even his intense desire to please her. Though her confession of abuse had avoided the bedroom, she had implied without actually saying it that sex hadn't been good between her and her ex-husband; it was something Mitch was certain of now. Her astonishment in his arms had told him that.

Even though need was riding him with a pulsing, bittersweet agony, he was aware of an almost savage satisfaction in that knowledge that was purely male and as old as time itself. No other man had seen her as he had, her delicate face taut with desire, her slender body writhing with need. No other man had heard the soft little sounds of uncontrolled passion, the final primitive cry of release. No other man could have felt the intense elation of having aroused her until she was at a point beyond herself, responding only to his touch.

The sharp talons of jealousy were less painful now, almost ghostly as they lost their hold on him. The man she had married had not won her heart or stirred her senses; for now it was enough.

All that was in him, the level of awareness almost beneath his conscious thoughts. But, even more, he was filled with another realization. He'd wanted to tell her, but hadn't been able to shape the words. When he'd first seen her in the bright light of the bedroom, her pale gold body naked for the first time, he'd wanted to say that sometimes reality did measure up to dreams. That sometimes it even surpassed dreams.

So hungry for her that he knew how starvation felt, he couldn't stop touching her, feeling her silky flesh beneath his hands and mouth. The strain of holding back had him on the fine edge of total insanity, but with his knowledge of the hard lesson of just how quickly and easily time itself could be stolen from him, he was even more driven to make love to her as if this would be his one and only chance.

Because it might well be.

Whatever fears she had harbored were gone now, and Mitch could neither see nor sense a ghost between them. Kelly was as totally involved in this as he was, completely responsive. He could feel her soft hands moving over his shoulders and back, feel the satiny skin of her inner thigh brush against his hip as she pressed herself closer.

"Mitch," she murmured throatily, gleaming eyes darkened to purple as she looked at him.

He kissed her deeply as he settled between her thighs but braced himself away from her, managing to hold back even though the need to bury himself in her was tearing him apart. She was ready for him, trying to draw him down into her softness, and he could feel the tension of building desire in her body. She was moving slightly beneath him, dazed purple eyes fixed on his face, her breasts rising and falling rapidly with her shallow breathing.

"Lord," he muttered, his control shattering as need surged through him like a hot red tide. "Oh, dear Lord, Kelly . . ." He had waited for her too long to be able to wait another second. He bore down slowly, the sensations of her tight heat enclosing him so exquisite that a groan of pleasure forced its way past his clenched teeth. He felt the silky brush of her inner thighs as her legs lifted to wrap around his hips, saw her eyes widen and then lose focus in a dreamy look so starkly, mysteriously feminine that it stole what was left of his breath.

Mitch wanted to make it last, but the need reined so tightly for so long burst free. He was aware of nothing except the woman cradling him, of the rising heat between them. She was with him all the way, her slender body responding to his powerful thrusts with lithe strength, the almost silent whimpering sounds she made driving his need higher and higher. Everything inside him began to rush wildly, like a molten flood sweeping through him. He barely heard her gasping cry, but the hot inner contractions of her pleasure caught him in delicate, sensuous ripples that pushed him violently over the edge and made a rasping groan tear from his throat.

The heavy weight of his body felt surprisingly comfortable to Kelly, and she didn't want him to move. Her own body was limp and astonishingly filled with satisfaction. Soft aftershocks of pleasure lingered deep inside her, and she found herself wondering if the delight she'd found in Mitch's arms was something so rare it could never be repeated. She hoped that wasn't true, because it was a part of loving him she found absolutely wonderful. She seemed to be floating, even with his weight holding her down, and the feeling was so exquisite that she didn't want to let go of it.

She felt sleep tugging at her mind, and thought vaguely that this time there would be no nightmares.

Nothing can take her away from me now. It was the first clear thought in Mitch's mind, and one he instantly pushed away. Not because he didn't want it to be true, but because he knew only too well how fickle fate truly was and had a superstitious compulsion not to tempt it. Concentrating on other things, he raised his upper body slightly and kissed her. Eyes still closed, she smiled and murmured something wordless, a sound of contentment. He started to ease away so that she'd be more comfortable, then changed his mind and rolled instead so that she lay on top of him.

She lifted her head briefly as if the new position startled her, but her eyes remained sleepy. "Mitch?"

"Go to sleep, sweetheart," he said huskily.

With another murmur she rested her cheek on his chest and went still, supple as a cat.

Drawing the covers up over their cooling bodies, he held her securely, one hand stroking her soft hair. The warm weight of her slender body was oddly reassuring, but even so he couldn't sleep himself. Though he should have been tired, he wasn't; he felt wide awake and was conscious that the sharp edge of his desire for her had merely been blunted. And the thoughts running through his mind were too clear to avoid.

She had been the focus of his life ten years earlier, and yet he had taken her for granted. So arrogantly certain he was in control of his destiny, it had never occurred to him that what he had felt for Kelly was something to cherish and protect, something he might be called upon to fight for. Something that could all too easily be taken away from him. He hadn't thought about it, hadn't understood at all how deeply and surely the emotions had run in him. Perhaps she was right in saying that then he had needed her to be unformed and dependent. But that explanation was far too simple to be all the truth, Mitch knew now.

Because nothing could have kept him away from her. Through all the long, painful months of therapy, his determination to find Kelly had been the only thing that had kept him going. Completely aware that ten years would have changed her just as the loss of years had changed him, he had known only that he had to find her. If it had taken him another ten years—or even a lifetime —he wouldn't have stopped searching. And if he had found her married, happily or not, he would have done his level best to take her away from that other man.

Arrogant? He examined the word, and knew it was the wrong one. *Desperate* was closer to the mark. Though his conscious reasoning had been complex and even confused, on a deeper level of himself, it had been implacable, certain.

He and Kelly belonged together. He felt it in his very bones, at the core of himself, a truth like a brand on his soul.

Mitch rubbed his chin in her soft hair and stared at the ceiling as his arms tightened around her. Ten years gone, yet they still had a chance. Still had a possible future—and maybe fate was responsible for that as well. Since awakening from the coma, he'd thought of fate as something hostile, a thief moving soundlessly in the night, but now he wondered if perhaps there was another side. Because what he felt for Kelly was too deeply rooted in himself to be something he had stumbled into by meeting her brother. Perhaps the destiny he had tried so hard to control had entangled him securely long before he had thought himself master of it.

Perhaps his destiny was to love Kelly. No matter what. Despite the vagaries of time and the whims of fate.

That he had always loved Kelly was an unnerving idea for a rational man. He had loved her always in this life . . . and always in whatever had come before. Or would come after.

But he didn't know how she felt. Between them there was no such thing as a "simple" emotion; the memories they shared over the years as well as all their losses made that an inevitable truth. She hadn't been able to let go of him, but what did that mean? Love or guilt? And would this new turn in their relationship provide answers, or more questions? Was she still convinced that all they had left together was an ending? Even now?

They were lovers now. *Whatever happens, I don't want to regret that again.* A chapter ended for Kelly, with no regrets of what might have been to haunt her?

His arms again tightened around her and he stared grimly at the ceiling. Arrogance, he thought, had its benefits; it had at least insulated him from this grinding uncertainty ten years earlier. But he couldn't afford arrogance today. He couldn't control time or fate . . . or even Kelly's love.

She stirred slightly and lifted her head from his chest, her peaceful nap over, and he forced his arms to relax. "Hi," he said softly, smiling.

Her eyes skittered away from his briefly, but it was a look of faint shyness rather than discomfort or regret. She cleared her throat with an uncertain sound, her gaze steady now and a bit questioning. "Hi. Did I fall asleep?"

"For a while."

"You didn't," she guessed.

"No. I have a little trouble with sleep these days."

The response had been matter-of-fact, but Kelly felt herself shudder with empathetic pain. "It's natural after what happened," she offered.

"So the doctors said." He shrugged as if to dismiss the subject, then lifted his head from the pillow and kissed her. Somewhere during that long, slow, heated kiss, he shifted position so that Kelly found herself lying on her back close beside him, her arms around his neck.

"I never knew," she whispered against his lips, the confession made because she wanted him to understand just how much pleasure she'd found in his arms. "I didn't even dream I could feel that way."

Mitch kissed her again, then searched her face with a gaze he knew was too intense. But he couldn't temper what he was feeling, because his own thoughts had made him afraid. Afraid he'd lose her again. "Sometimes reality is better than dreams. And the reality is that we belong together, Kelly."

"Do we?" She avoided his gaze. "Because of ten years ago?"

"Because of now. Can't you feel that?"

She *did* feel it—but she didn't trust the emotions. They were still tangled inside her, and she needed time to sort them out. "Mitch, it has all happened so fast. I'm not sure what I feel. I know only that ten years is a long time, and not something we can ignore. You said that I had to come to you because I wanted to, not because I felt guilty. We both have to be sure of that. Any doubt could destroy us."

He took a slow, deep breath and then nodded slightly. "You're right, I know. I'm trying, Kelly. I'm trying not to hold on to you too hard."

Looking up at the lean, handsome face that had tautened with his emotions, Kelly felt as much as saw what this meant to him. It wasn't just important, it was vital. And it disturbed her on some deep level to realize she could be so much a part of someone else's happiness. He saw her reaction, and his face relaxed suddenly.

"I'm sorry, sweetheart." His voice was rueful. "I didn't mean to overwhelm you. I think I did that once before."

Grateful for the crooked smile that invited her to share his wry look back at his younger self, she lifted her eyebrows and made her own voice dry. "You certainly did. Gathering my family together and announcing briskly that we were going to be married as soon as I graduated. If I'd been a little older, I probably would have thrown something at you."

"Believe me, I don't *want* to be domineering. If I say or do anything that feels that way to you, tell me. All right?"

She nodded, smiling a little. "All right. But now it's my turn to warn you."

He eyed her warily. "Oh?"

"Yes. I am older now, Mitch."

He chuckled softly. "I'll get ready to duck." He bent his head and kissed her, the first light touch rapidly heating and becoming more deliberate.

Kelly pressed herself closer, her hands stroking his thick dark hair and her mouth coming alive beneath his. A sound of pleasure purred in the back of her throat, and she gave herself up to the wonder of these incredible feelings.

It was some considerable time later when they shared a shower in the glassed-in stall, and Kelly's initial stiffness faded in the face of his behavior. Mitch looked at her and touched her, his intense yet tender expression as well as his murmured words telling her clearly that he found her beautiful. And though she very obviously aroused him—the interlude in the shower left her with the vague, curiously delighted certainty that all her bones had melted away—he never made her feel as if her body were only a source of physical satisfaction for him and nothing else.

He helped her to dry off, dropping occasional kisses on rosy flesh, the caresses definitely stirring her blood yet just as definitely intended to be soothing and loving rather than arousing.

They were new lovers physically, but the feelings that had prompted this new turn in their relationship were longstanding ones. And their reaction to each other now was a curious mixture of both. She was still a little shy, a little surprised but pleased by his fascination in the shape of her, the textures of her body. At the same time, Mitch had been a part of her for so long that her responses to him seemed to come from deep inside herself and without thought. And he touched her with an odd sense of familiarity as well as fascination.

Kelly got clean underwear out of the bureau in the bathroom and put it on, then went into the bedroom, where Mitch was putting on his discarded clothing. He eyed her as she pulled jeans and a bulky sweater from the chest of drawers, and when he spoke his voice was both light and husky.

"That ought to be illegal."

"What?" she asked, turning to look at him.

"Frilly underwear."

She glanced down at the flesh-colored bra and panties, which were lace-edged but otherwise rather plain, and laughed. "This? I have some lingerie that's a lot more adventurous."

He grinned slightly, looking extremely piratical as he stood there buttoning his shirt. "I hope you mean to do some adventuring," he said. "I've seen a few outfits in store windows and imagined you in them. Talk about fantasizing."

Kelly stepped into her jeans and drew them up. "Frederick's of Hollywood—type stuff?" she asked dryly.

"I have no idea. I wasn't exactly paying attention to advertising. I remember one red lace thing with garters, and there was something in black that looked like one of those old-fashioned corsets."

Choking back a laugh, she pulled the bulky sweater over her head. "You must have spent a lot of time in front of that window. Didn't you get odd looks from passersby?"

"One little old lady snorted at me in disgust."

"Ladies don't snort, they sniff."

"This one," Mitch said with feeling, "snorted. And she made straight for a cop standing nearby on the street, obviously to report me as a pervert. So I slunk away, hugging my fantasies close."

Her earlier thoughts came back to haunt her as she wondered suddenly about fantasies—and realities. She turned toward the dresser, running a brush through her damp hair, then put on her wristwatch. And, automatically, picked up the thin chain she always removed at night, slipping it over her head and allowing the ring to rest inside her sweater.

"Hey," Mitch said in a wounded tone, "you were supposed to laugh."

"At the image of you slinking away?" she asked lightly. "I think the lady was rude for intruding on your fantasies."

"What's wrong, sweetheart?"

She looked up to meet his gaze in the mirror, watching as he came up behind her and slipped his arms around her waist. Drawn back against the hard warmth of his body, she struggled not to ask what she had no right to. "Wrong?"

"Something's bothering you. What is it?"

Kelly managed a shrug. "It's nothing. Gremlins of the mind. And none of my business."

Mitch smiled. "Oh. Other women?"

She frowned at him in the mirror, trying to keep it light. "Was I that obvious?"

"It must have been this connection of ours," Mitch murmured, still smiling.

"Teenagers are so complacent," she offered, determined to sound offhand and merely thoughtful. "It just occurred to me recently that it *never* occurred to me then. I mean, there you were in your twenties, according to all the studies at the peak of your sexuality, and I was determined to be a virgin bride. Three years engaged, and I never even considered the possibility that you might have . . ."

"Stepped out on you?"

She laughed suddenly, honestly, if ruefully, amused. "It is ridiculous, isn't it? To have expected you to wait three years so I could wear white without guilt." A sudden memory made her add in a dry tone, "I should have known better. You and Keith were chasing girls all through your teens, and I know you caught quite a few of them. It used to make me feel miserable to see you with your arm around some busty blonde." The arms currently around her tightened slightly, and in the mirror his expression looked curiously indecisive.

"I was a normal teenager," he admitted lightly. "Hormones raging, bent on conquest. And there were a few girls in those days."

"Of course there were," she agreed in a brisk tone, forcing herself to ignore the painful stab of unreasoning jealousy she had no right to feel. "Like I said, anything else would have been ridiculous."

"There were a few girls," he repeated deliberately, the brief look of indecision gone from his expression, "before you, Kelly. Not after."

She turned in his arms so that she could look up at his face rather than at his reflection. Her hands lifted to rest on his hard chest. "What?" She felt a little numb. Surely he didn't mean . . .

Mitch kept his arms around her, but loosely now. Obviously trying to lessen the impact of what he was saying, he kept his voice light and rather thoughtful. "Half your life, but I can't really say it was fourteen years, since I was unconscious for nine of them. And for the better part of this past year I didn't have the strength or the inclination to chase nurses—no doubt because I was hardly in what you'd call prime physical condition, and because none of them was you. So we'll say it was four and a half years, give or take a couple of months."

Kelly swallowed hard. "You mean . . . even after you came out of the coma, you didn't—?"

"Doctors," Mitch said consideringly, "love to explain things in clinical terms. And my doctors, including the physical therapists, were careful to explain that there'd been no injuries that would prohibit my enjoying an active, healthy sex life. At the time I was too concerned with getting back on my feet to think about it very much."

She stared at him.

With an expression that was both humorous and rather self-mockingly defensive, he said, "All right, I *did* think about it. You weren't there, though, and I decided—well, I decided that was the problem. But the coma had stolen several other things, after all, and I couldn't be sure. Still, I kept telling myself everything would be fine. The entire point of the therapy was to get all my muscles and nerves back in working order, so I could hardly expect . . ."

Kelly had a good idea of why Mitch was being humorous and mocking about this, and it wasn't only to cover what must certainly have been a very real anxiety. She was so moved she could hardly bear it, and yet at the same time she was conscious of a giggle trapped in the back of her throat. It was the *way* he was explaining this to her, with that disarming charm of his she remembered so well, his lean face so expressively droll. As if the whole thing, at least with the benefit of hindsight, were absolutely ludicrous.

She wasn't sure if she wanted to hug him, hit him, or shake him.

"Everybody kept telling me I was doing fine," he went on in a thoughtful tone. "Just remarkable, they said. No problems and nothing at all for me to worry about. And I didn't really have the nerve to say, hey, Doc, I think the family jewels are lagging behind."

Kelly bit her bottom lip, and carefully cleared her throat. She wasn't going to laugh. She *wasn't.* "I—I see. And—when you got out of the hospital?"

"I fixed all my attention on finding you. I didn't want anyone else, so I figured that was the problem anyway. When I first got here, the emotions were so thick, they sort of got in the way of a physical response. But, then, the next morning . . . the possibility was definitely there."

She suddenly remembered that morning, and his intense scrutiny of her. She'd felt his desire then, so sharp and powerful it had badly unnerved her. "Oh," she murmured.

Mitch eyed her severely. "Oh? Is that all you have to say? Talk about waking the dead."

Kelly choked, and balled up one fist to punch him somewhat weakly on the chest. "Stop making me laugh! You aren't fooling me into believing it wasn't serious to you."

"I was hoping you wouldn't realize that. You know what they say about fragile male egos?"

"I've heard a few things."

"They're all true," he said sheepishly.

This time she managed not to laugh. And, since she knew the other reason he had guided her along the deliberately humorous path of his worries about the "family jewels," she forced herself to face the central fact about which he had so carefully been offhanded.

"But not really the point, I think," she said steadily. "The point is that you waited for me. And I didn't wait for you."

Seven

"Dammit, this is just what I didn't want to happen." All signs of self-mocking humor were gone; Mitch's face was entirely serious and even a little grim.

"I can't avoid the truth," she said.

"You're painting the truth with guilt," he told her flatly. "And there's no reason. Kelly, stop and think about it for a minute. That arrogance of mine, remember? I could afford to be noble and wait while you grew up because there was never any doubt in my mind. We were going to spend the rest of our lives together, I *knew* that. So what if I was so horny I had to take long walks and cold showers? I didn't want another woman, I wanted you. Hell, I congratulated myself on being so patient."

"You did?" she asked involuntarily.

He laughed shortly. "Of course I did. Combine the sins of arrogance with a sense of one's own superiority, and that was me. I was the so-called adult, remember, waiting for my child bride to become a woman. And I was so damned sure of myself, it took a kick from fate to knock me on my backside."

With the wind taken out of her sails, Kelly stared up at him. "So you're saying you waited for me with the worst of motives, and I left you with the best of them?"

Some of the grimness faded from his face, and Mitch smiled. "Does sound a bit cut and dried, but that's basically it. I loved you, Kelly, and the waiting was easier because of that. But the truth—the bare truth not painted with guilt or anything at all—is that I knew we'd have a future together, and you knew we wouldn't."

"But you're here—"

His hands slid up to grasp her shoulders, and he shook her gently. "Stop saying that. It's a fluke that I'm here, a whim of fate. One of the rare little jokes God probably uses to teach medical science they don't know as much as they think they do. The point is that nobody thought I'd wake up. Nobody, sweetheart."

Kelly accepted that for the moment. But she knew the question of her guilt was yet to be settled. Because no matter how convincing his arguments were, the fact was that Mitch was still unable to forgive her. Maybe that sense of betrayal he'd been so honest about *was* deeply buried, and maybe he could come to terms with it—but he hadn't yet. And unless and until he did, she couldn't completely forgive herself.

She pushed it aside for now. She wanted to be happy today, to delight in the closeness between them. Conjuring a smile, she said, "Well, you didn't have to try to make me laugh over your worry that you were—"

He kissed her quickly. "Don't say it. I wouldn't even let myself say that word."

"All right, I won't say it. Besides, you're fine now."

Mitch eyed her. "Fine?"

She studied him with a mock frown. "Are we dealing with a fragile ego here?"

"I just thought that *fine* was sort of a lackluster word to use," he explained in a pained tone.

Kelly bit her lip, then said, "I suppose from your point of view it might have been."

"Naturally. If you'd said magnificent, now, or stupendous, I might have felt a bit more secure. But *fine*? Fine is what you are when you've gotten over a cold. Fine is not what you are after experiencing major emotional trauma."

She rested her forehead against his chest and allowed the pent-up giggles to escape. It felt wonderful.

"Now she's laughing at me," Mitch said in a depressed tone with a thread of amusement woven through it. "The woman is running amok over my ego. If I had any arrogance left, it is writhing in the dust."

"I'd forgotten you could be so funny," she murmured into his shirt.

"Funny? Light of my life, years from now, when they speak of this, and they will, they'll say—"

"They?"

"Quiet, I'm being lyrical."

"Pardon me, I'm sure."

"They'll say . . . what will they say? Oh, yes. They'll say, 'She trod carelessly upon the dark insecurity of her man, laying bare with a single four-letter word that consuming fear every male hides deep in his ego. She said *fine*, and his very soul quivered under the blow.'"

Kelly lifted a solemn face from the front of his shirt. "Will they let me have a second chance?" she asked meekly.

"If you grovel."

Reflectively, she said, "I'd rather just stand here proudly and correct this sad misapprehension you seem to be laboring under."

Mitch linked his fingers together at the small of her back and looked magnanimous. "I'm listening."

"Then I'll say, in all truth, that these last hours—" She looked at her watch and remarked in mild surprise, "It's almost noon. Did you know that?"

He gave her a little shake and growled.

Kelly cleared her throat hastily. "As I was saying, these last hours have been so utterly wonderful that mere words are hopelessly inadequate to describe them."

Mitch waited a beat, then frowned at her.

"Well, they are." She sobered abruptly and stood on tiptoe to curve her arms around his neck. "Even magnificent and stupendous fall short of the mark."

He hugged her. "Hey, if you're going to get serious, we'd better go downstairs and rustle up some food. Obviously, you're in a weakened condition."

She kissed his chin, knowing that he was fully aware of the pleasure she'd found in his arms. "Obviously."

Mitch chuckled and held her hand firmly as they left the bedroom and started downstairs. "Are you going to insist on working today?"

Kelly felt a stab of guilt, and gave him a slightly worried look. "I really should, at least for a couple of hours. I need to call Mr. Fortune and check a few things with him."

"I'm not going to kick and scream about it," Mitch told her dryly. "But I do think you've been working too hard the last few days. To avoid me, I know."

She smiled. "It showed, huh?"

"Around the edges. I probably learned a valuable lesson in patience."

They had reached the kitchen by then, and as she went to look in the refrigerator she said lightly, "A useful virtue to cultivate. Should I be listening for the other shoe to drop?"

He had no difficulty in understanding the mild question. In the same tone she'd used, he said, "It's obviously going to take time for you to believe it, but no. I can't be the same man I used to be, Kelly. Even if I wanted to. If I try to hold on to you too tightly, it won't be out of domination or arrogance—but out of fear."

She turned to look at him, but he gestured slightly before she could speak.

"I know, that motive's hardly a better one. But I can't pretend it isn't there. The fear of loss is something—something I may never overcome." His matter-of-fact voice didn't quite conceal the emotions beneath. "But it is something I'm aware of, something I can consciously control. Kelly, if I've learned anything through all this, it's that you can't build walls around the people you care about. You can't do it to keep them near or to keep them safe. Even if they could stand the prison, that kind of control is still an illusion. To fate, the walls are made of air."

Kelly crossed the space between them and slid her arms around his waist. "You are different," she murmured against his chest as his arms closed about her. "Before, you never talked about your feelings. You just—well, seemed to think I should understand without being told."

"I was a silly bastard," he said calmly, and kissed the tip of her nose as she looked up at him. "But I'm all grown-up now, and quite delighted with the woman you are. So stop listening for that other shoe; I've thrown it out the window. You may catch me in an odd moment trying to get my own way, but I think we can both deal with that."

She smiled. "I think so too."

"Good." He patted her bottom and then released her.

After lunch Kelly reluctantly went into her study to work. She admitted to herself that she would have preferred to spend the rest of the day with Mitch; after what had happened to them before, she was aware of a superstitious urge to remain as close to him as possible. But, just as he knew he couldn't hold on too tightly to her because of fear of loss, she knew the same was true for her. Still, knowing it did little to make her feel better.

It was so easy to mock fate. At least, as Mitch had more colorfully stated, until it kicked you where you hurt. With so much beyond any individual's control, it was almost terrifying to realize that control over even one's own future was very much in doubt.

A fact, however, was a fact, and had to be accepted. Kelly knew that wasn't the reason she had been unable to tell Mitch she loved him. It was because she wasn't yet whole. There was still, at the core of herself, some wavering uncertainty she hadn't been prepared to examine closely until now. She loved him, and she wanted them to be together. If he could forgive her for leaving him.

Was that it? She wasn't sure. Maybe. Partly, at

least. And partly because she was in a kind of limbo.

The thought stopped abruptly in her head, but Kelly made herself look at it squarely. She *was* in a kind of limbo, because Brad was still out there somewhere and a part of her was waiting for him to make a move. That, too, was something unfinished—and had to be handled.

She'd almost forgotten about him. Had forgotten about him for a while. Mitch had said very little about the possibility of her ex-husband showing up, but she knew it wasn't something he was ignoring. He had believed her, had accepted her belief that Brad meant to kill her if he could. But it struck her for the first time that Mitch *had* been unnaturally quiet about that possibility. He had changed, yes, but the man he was today was a stronger, tougher man in many ways—and hardly likely to sit and twiddle his thumbs if even the possibility of danger lurked nearby.

After a long, thoughtful moment, Kelly turned on her computer and prepared to work. She had a question to ask him, but there was no hurry.

Mitch held the receiver to his ear and frowned unseeingly across the kitchen as he listened to Evan Boyd's voice.

"Nothing was happening. I started getting the feeling that somebody was toying with us," the investigator was saying. "So I got a friend of mine in Texas to do a bit more checking on that out-of-the-country trip West was supposed to be on."

"And?" Mitch asked.

"It wasn't easy. Since West is in the travel business, he knows all the tricks. As far as we could determine, he didn't leave the country. But he didn't come here either."

"Where is he now?"

"That's the kicker. My friend hasn't actually seen him, but there have been at least two notices in the town's newspaper during the past three days that put him at charity functions right there. Nowhere near California or here. So I called his office, and was told that he was in a meeting. It could be the standard secretary's excuse, of course."

Mitch was silent for a moment, then he said, "What does your gut say?"

Sighing, Boyd replied, "My gut isn't saying a damned thing. Would the bastard be this devious?"

"I don't know. Maybe he hasn't tracked her this far yet. She told me that after moving to a new place it was usually weeks—even months—before he showed up. It could be that he doesn't know she's here."

The investigator sighed again. "The two guys I hired think we're both crazy, and they're bored; they aren't as good as I'd hoped. The cops told me to yell if something happened, but otherwise aren't interested. Look—maybe he *was* here and realized we were waiting for him. He could have decided to back off until the odds were better."

Flatly, Mitch said, "I won't look over my shoulder for the rest of my life, and I don't want Kelly to have to. If we can find out for certain where West is, I'll have *him* watched, twenty-four hours a day if necessary, until I can find a way to get him out of our lives for good."

"All right," Boyd said. "Then I'll fly down to Texas and eyeball him myself. I can probably get a flight sometime tomorrow. Do you want the other two to stay on watch?"

"How effective are they?" Mitch asked bluntly.

"Not very," the investigator admitted. "If West drives up to the front door in a tank, they'd probably spot him. They're good men—it's just that they don't feel a threat and that makes them slack."

"Then they're useless to me. Pay them off and send me the bill. I'll try to keep Kelly inside the house with the security system activated, at least until I hear from you again."

"I'll be as quick as I can."

"Fine. If he's in Texas, either watch him yourself or hire someone you trust to do it."

"You've got it."

Mitch cradled the receiver and turned around. She was leaning back against the doorjamb, her empty coffee cup dangling from one finger, face calm and eyes unreadable.

"Isn't it handy there are two phone lines into the house?" she asked.

He cleared his throat. "Are you mad at me?"

The direct question was curiously boyish, and Kelly was tempted to let him believe she was angry just to see how he'd react. But she shook her head. "No. It just occurred to me that you were being a bit too quiet about a possible threat, and I was going to ask you about that. I gather that was your investigator you were talking to? And that you've had the house watched for some time now?"

"It seemed . . . prudent," Mitch said cautiously.

"You should have told me."

He moved to stand in front of her, his hands lifting to rest on her shoulders. "I'm sorry. I think I didn't because . . . I didn't want to talk about him. I still don't, but I guess we have to." He drew a short breath. "I want him out of our lives, Kelly, for good. I don't want you to be afraid anymore.

That is part of the problem, isn't it? Between us, I mean. You can't think of the future because he's a threat."

Since she had just faced that fact herself, Kelly could hardly deny it. "It's . . . something I can't forget. Something that isn't finished."

His hands tightened gently on her shoulders. "We can stop him, sweetheart. We'll find a way. But right now I just want to make sure he's nowhere near you. Boyd is flying to Texas to make sure he's there, and he'll be watched."

She looked up at him, then nodded. "Just don't try to wrap me in cotton, all right, Mitch? That kind of protectiveness feels wonderful, but it's a crutch too. I have to stand on my own two feet."

He chuckled. "The instincts are old, you know. Stamped in the genes. But I'll do my best."

Kelly extended her free hand to touch his cheek as she returned his smile. "I can't ask for more, can I?"

"You can ask for anything." He kissed her lightly, adding, "Finished work for the day?"

She accepted the changed subject. "I have to call Mr. Fortune. It shouldn't take long."

The rest of the day was spent quietly, and the tentative moments between them gradually vanished as the barriers came down. Kelly realized that she was finally seeing Mitch clearly as the man he was today; her occasional comparisons between then and now became fewer and virtually unimportant. And she knew that he had also found a merging of past and present in her. Maybe the fact that they had become lovers had provided the bridge, or perhaps it was simply that they had at last worked their way across the distance between them, carefully, a step at a time.

Kelly had never before known true intimacy with a man; the months with Brad, even ,in the beginning, had made her feel anxious and unsure of herself, and since she'd been unable to respond to him physically—something he had adamantly insisted was her fault—she had felt like a failure as a woman. Her response to Mitch, so instant and powerful, gave her a new confidence that brought her out of herself.

She wasn't fully aware of her own sensual blooming until that night. During the hours before they had climbed the stairs together, Mitch had touched her a great deal, not casually but without demand, and she had loved that closeness. Kissing her, stroking her back, holding her hand. His obvious pleasure in just touching her allowed her the freedom to explore and enjoy the intimacy between lovers.

And by the time they stepped into the lamplit quiet of the big master bedroom, she could feel the inner pressure of desire that had been building slowly. She caught her breath when he slipped his arms around her and eased her against his hard body, very aware of his pulsing hunger.

"Oh, Lord, what you do to me," he murmured against her mouth, his hands sliding down over her bottom to hold her even closer. "I can't keep my hands off you."

Kelly's arms curved up around his neck as she melted against him. "You make me feel so . . ."

He kissed her deeply, exploring her mouth with a slow intensity until a wordless sound of pleasure purred in the back of her throat. Then he lifted his head and looked down at her dazed eyes. "So . . . what?" he asked.

She concentrated on the need to form a word. "Sexy," she managed to say at last. More words came, husky and unsteady. "I've never felt that way before." She drew in a sharp breath when he moved subtly against her, her eyes widening and then drifting half shut. "I can't control it."

"Do you think I can?" He kissed her again, harder this time, and his intent expression tautened when her legs parted to allow him to be even closer. "It's like a hunger I can never satisfy, an aching that fades but never goes away. I have to be inside you, feel the silky tightness of you around me, so soft and hot and wet I think I'm going out of my mind."

The rough words and slow movements against her sent the last of Kelly's clear thoughts spinning away. When his mouth covered hers she kissed him back wildly, every thudding beat of her heart causing the pressure inside her to build until her entire body seemed to pulse with throbbing need. She almost cried out in disappointment when he eased back away from her, but when he swiftly unbuttoned his shirt and impatiently threw it aside, she reached to get rid of her own clothing. Her hands were shaking so badly that he had to help her unfasten her jeans and push the heavy material down over her hips. Her panties followed to join the shoes and clothing kicked aside and jumbled on the floor. And it was Mitch who lifted the thin chain from around her neck and dropped it onto the dresser.

To her vague surprise, Mitch sank down on the edge of the bed and drew her naked body down to straddle his lap, but she forgot her startlement when his mouth slanted hotly over hers. He was holding her tightly, his hands stroking up and down her spine in a tingling caress, and she could feel the pulsating hardness of him pressed against her belly. Instinctively, she squirmed to be even closer to him, the sensual tension building inside her like pain that surged and ebbed and surged again.

A groan rumbled in his chest as his lips trailed down over her throat. He kept one arm around her waist and bent her back slightly, his other hand sliding up over her rib cage and cupping a swelling breast. Kelly clutched his shoulders and bit her lip as he lifted and kneaded her aching flesh, sharp jolts of pleasure stabbing through her. The rough pad of his thumb brushed her tight nipple rhythmically, making her quiver like a live wire, and his mouth explored the satiny slope of her breast with a wet heat that was driving her mad.

Her back arched and her nails dug into his hard shoulders, a whimper escaping her. She was burning alive, her mind submerged in the fire. His slow caresses had so sensitized her flesh that when his mouth closed over her stiff nipple she didn't know if what she felt was pleasure or agony. Her entire body jerked and a moan tore from her throat. Eyes tightly closed, her head thrown back, she endured the waves of feeling because she had no choice, because it was a terrible pleasure her body craved.

She had no self-control. It was a dim realization, almost instantly swamped by pure need. Her body had a mind of its own, and it wanted only him. To be filled by him, because the emptiness hurt so much. She writhed against him, hardly recognizing the thin sound of her own voice.

"Please . . . Mitch, I can't . . ."

With another rough sound he lifted his mouth from her aching breasts. His big hands slid beneath her bottom, raising her, and she moaned when she felt the blunt heat of his flesh parting hers and easing inside her.

"Look at me, sweetheart," he whispered, his voice nearly gone.

She forced her eyes open, finding his face blurred at first but then clear and sharp, his features masklike and excitingly primitive, the dark eye burning. He was still holding her so that he was just barely inside her and she could scarcely stand it. She couldn't breathe, her heart was pounding wildly and her body was shuddering, and he was *killing* her—

Then, staring into his intense gaze, she felt him slowly lowering her, pushing deep inside her until he filled the emptiness that craved him.

"So beautiful," he said in that cracked, hoarse whisper. "So beautiful like this, wanting me." His hands guided her in slow movements as his mouth brushed her trembling lips again and again, always lifting his head after each teasing nibble to watch her face. She could feel the waves inside her quickening, rushing, the sound of them leaving her in whimpers she was helpless to hold back. Her body found its own rhythm, wild with need, and she could dimly hear the sounds she made, some wordless and some only his name, tearing free of her.

She was almost sobbing when Mitch stood up and tumbled her limp body back onto the bed, and he couldn't hold back any longer. He'd managed to until then only because he'd been so intent on watching and feeling her pleasure, totally fascinated by the way her eyes went unfocused and her face became a beautiful mask of passion, by the way her body rippled and pulsed as it held him tightly inside her. But now he was wild for her, his own need taking over as he slid his hands beneath her and lifted her for each deep thrust. He caught her pleasure before it could ebb, and sensual tension built rapidly in her again as she matched his passionate rhythm.

Every harsh breath he drew was fire in his lungs; it was like some mad race he had to win or die trying. And she was so soft and hot around him, her legs lifting to cradle him, a tiny heartbeat throbbing violently under the silken skin of her neck when he pressed his mouth there. He felt the first electric tremors near the base of his spine, and heard her cry out as he buried himself in her writhing body.

It was a long time before his ragged breathing steadied, and even then Mitch didn't think he had the strength to move. He knew damned well he didn't have the strength to leave her. He wanted to stay right where he was, still inside her, where the soft, ebbing ripples of satisfaction caressed him gently. He felt her move slightly as she lifted her head from the pillow to kiss his shoulder, and made himself raise his own head and then ease himself up on his elbows.

Her delicate face was pale with the totally drained look of sensual exhaustion, a glowing pallor. Lips that were faintly swollen from his kisses were curved in a slight smile, and her purple eyes were solemn.

"I need a thesaurus," she murmured.

"What?" His mind scrambled to figure that out. "Why?"

"There must," she said, still solemn, "be better

words than *magnificent* and *stupendous*. Because, if there aren't—I'm going to invent a few."

He had to laugh a little, even as he kissed her gently. "I love you, honey."

For the first time, that endearment awoke no memories of how another man had dirtied it. She felt a dim shock, but only because he'd said that he loved her. Her. Not the girl he had loved years before, but the woman she was now. She had felt his love, seen it in his gaze, his smile, but she hadn't really let herself believe that he could fall in love with her twice.

She swallowed hard. "Was—was it only this morning that I said everything had happened too fast?" she murmured.

Mitch kissed her again. "I had to say it." His voice roughened suddenly. "It's what I've been feeling all along. Changing and growing because I didn't know you enough at first, but always there. Kelly, I'm not bitter that you walked away from me. I can't blame you for that, and I don't. I can even be glad about it now, because if you hadn't, I might never have known what an incredible woman you could become."

"You forgive me?"

"There's nothing to forgive. I mean that, sweetheart. I'm so damned grateful I got another chance with you; that's all that matters now."

Kelly wanted to tell him that she loved him, but the words wouldn't emerge. Brad was still out there, still casting a shadow over her future, and that had to be finished.

She didn't know what Mitch saw in her face, but whatever it was, it made his own expression soften.

"It's all right, honey."

"Is it?" she whispered, her arms tightening around his neck. "I want it to be, Mitch. Oh, Lord, I want it to be."

He kissed her gently, then with a slowly deepening force. Heat washed over her in waves, and she forgot about being weary, about being unable to tell him she loved him. She forgot about everything except him.

She woke very early the next morning to find his arms wrapped around her. Not painfully, but she knew she wouldn't be able to pull away without waking him. She lifted her head from his shoulder, reluctant to disturb him. He hadn't slept well, she knew. He hadn't gotten out of bed or moved restlessly, but several times she had been dimly aware that he had jerked awake. Each time, only half awake herself, she had instinctively pressed closer to him and had felt his arms tighten around her as he relaxed.

Now, looking at his peaceful and unaware face, she wondered if he could ever trust sleep again. Awake, he could fight his innate possessiveness, but in sleep he could not. Sleep had stolen too much from him already.

Kelly felt that she could somehow help heal him, but only when she was healed herself. When she could love him without reservation. And she wouldn't be able to do that until Brad was out of her life for good.

Mitch stiffened suddenly as he woke, his arms tightening almost painfully around her, and she felt her heart turn over at the brief flash of dread she saw in his eye. Then he looked at her, and his arms slowly relaxed.

"I'm sorry," he said huskily. "I didn't mean to hold you so tightly."

"I don't mind being held in the night," she whispered. "Maybe we both need that . . . that feeling of security."

One of his hands slid up her spine to the nape of her neck, and he drew her forward so that he could kiss her. After a few moments he murmured, "It isn't security I'm feeling now."

Kelly knew what he was feeling, and there was a deep sense of wonder in her both for his desire and her own instant response. When he had finally turned out the lamp the night before, she'd been convinced that she would never be able to move again. She'd been so sated and exhausted that even opening her eyes had required too much strength. But now the soreness in her muscles vanished, and strength flowed into them.

It was a wonderful way to greet a new day.

When she slipped carefully from the bed an hour later, Mitch was sleeping deeply. She'd finally worn him out, poor baby. Kelly grinned to herself at the thought; it was both strange and marvelous to enjoy the feelings he aroused in her, and she was delighted by that sensual pleasure. He had not only taught her to enjoy lovemaking, but made her feel utterly comfortable with her own body.

A body which, as she straightened beside the bed, twinged faintly in several areas. Knowing that a hot shower would take most of the soreness out of her muscles, she went into the bathroom and eased the door shut so that she wouldn't wake Mitch. She put her hair up and took a shower, luxuriating in the feeling of hot water flowing down over her body.

She felt alive. Vividly, starkly alive.

Maybe that was why, after she'd gotten out of the stall and dried off, she opened the bottom drawer of the bureau. In here were the more "adventurous" items of lingerie she owned, all bought after her marriage, when she'd discovered a liking for silk and lace against her skin. She pulled on a sheer black silk camisole and matching panties, wondering if the outfit was the kind of thing that had inspired Mitch's fantasies in front of the store window, and hoping it was.

He was still asleep when she slipped cautiously back into the bedroom. Swiftly but quietly, she dressed in jeans and a midnight-blue blouse, deliberately leaving the first two buttons of the blouse unfastened so that a hint of black silk was visible. She took her hair down and brushed it, and then found her shoes in the jumble still lying on the floor.

She went to the bed and sat down on the edge, gazing at him. The tumbled covers had fallen to his waist, leaving his broad, hard chest bare, and she had to resist an impulse to throw off her clothes and climb back into bed with him. Instead, she leaned over and kissed him.

Even before he was fully awake, Mitch was responding, his arms reaching for her. She straightened before he could get hold of her, and smiled down at him. "Good morning."

He looked at her. "You're dressed." It was an accusation.

"I'm in a weakened condition again," she explained, "and I need to be fed. I was hoping I could persuade you to fix a batch of those delicious waffles."

"I suppose. . . . What are you wearing under that blouse?" he demanded suddenly.

Kelly got to her feet and stretched languidly. "Something adventurous. I think."

For a moment his expression was—peculiar. Somewhere between bemused and fiercely male.

Casually, she said, "I'm going to go down and start the coffee. It should be ready by the time you shave and get dressed."

Mitch cleared his throat. "You're an evil woman."

Kelly got her coffee, but the waffles were a bit delayed. By the time Mitch joined her in the conservatory nearly an hour later, he wasn't in the mood to cook.

Eight

"Such a pretty sight."

The voice was deep and pleasant, but Kelly felt her blood turn to ice at the sound of it. The fear she had lived with for so long awoke and crawled inside her, tearing at her will, her self-respect, reducing her to a cornered animal. She wanted to fold in on herself, to hide.

Stupid. She'd been stupid to just walk out of the house, but danger hadn't been in her mind; for the first time in nearly three years, she hadn't been on guard. Mitch had gone to find out if the attic still held the old trunk filled with his family's photographs and private letters, and she'd wandered out through the conservatory without even thinking about it, going down into the lower garden. She'd found herself pruning dead leaves off a tangled rose shrub and thinking idly that it would be beautiful when spring finally came. The late-morning sunshine was so bright and warm—

It didn't feel very warm now.

"Turn around and look at your husband, honey."

His voice was sharper now, the endearment dripping with contempt. So different from Mitch. So different. She forced herself to turn, to look at him, vaguely aware of the distant sound of a phone ringing in the house.

He was a big man, several inches over six feet, and powerfully built. He had played football in college, and kept in shape since by lifting weights. She knew how strong he was. Average in appearance other than his size, he had fair hair and deceptively mild blue eyes, and a wide white smile that tended to dazzle people. It had dazzled her.

The smile wasn't in evidence now. His thin lips were a grim slash in his beard-stubbled face, and red-rimmed eyes looked hot and mean. The gun held negligently in his hand was outsized and threatening, just as he was. It was a big silver weapon, and some distant whisper of knowledge told her that one shot could probably cut a person in half.

"You look so surprised, honey," he said in the gentle tone that had always preceded brutality. "Weren't you expecting me? I always knew you'd end up here in your lover's house. It was just a matter of time, so of course I waited."

Kelly swallowed the huge lump of terror in her throat, but her voice was still choked when it emerged. "Leave me alone. Why can't you leave me alone."

"You shouldn't have left me, honey. I told you I keep what belongs to me. You're my wife."

"I divorced you," she whispered.

His eyes narrowed. "You think a piece of paper means anything? You're mine. I made you mine, remember?" He laughed suddenly, harshly. "Oh, don't shrink back like some timid virgin, honey.

You put on a good act with me and turned up your nose like sex was something only the animals did, but I've watched you with him. Rubbing up against him like a cat in heat. You can't keep your hands off him."

In her reeling mind was a single sickening realization. "You watched?"

Brad didn't seem to hear. "With me you were so cold I could hear the ice crack when you moved. And flannel nightgowns from neck to ankle, nothing like that black silk thing you wore for him. He should have rotted away like a vegetable in that hospital, but you kept him alive, didn't you? His ghost in my bed, and you wouldn't let go of him, wouldn't let the bastard die. I would have beat him out of you, but you ran before I could finish the job."

"Stop." There was something else inside her now, twisting and churning, something stronger than fear.

He laughed again. "I've just been biding my time, honey. I knew he'd come back from the dead. It was amusing to watch you run like a scared rabbit, and it was just a matter of time before he woke up and came looking for you. I knew he would. And I knew you'd welcome him into your bed. I wanted to see the two of you together before I sent you both to hell. Wasn't that nice of me? I've let you finally have your ghost, and right where you wanted him too—between your legs."

"*Stop.*"

His face hardened. "You shouldn't have threatened me, Kelly. Nobody threatens me. I let you get away with it in Texas because that big-mouth lawyer you hired meant to make a circus out of our private affairs. He wanted to pin an assault rap on me and wail about how I beat up my poor little wife. But I got rid of the pictures in his dinky safe; your evidence is ashes, honey. And I've got witnesses to say I'm at home right now. The perfect crime. I'll blow my cheating wife and her lover to hell, and nobody'll ever know it was me."

The threat of death, curiously, was something she hardly paid attention to. She heard herself speak as if from a great distance, that churning thing inside her growing larger. "You watched us. In the conservatory."

"Quite a show you put on," he said, but despite the light words his face twitched in sheer rage. "I always knew you were a whore at heart—the frigid ones never fool me. Well, he's had you, but he won't keep you. I'll see you in hell, honey."

She wasn't even looking at the gun. She was staring at his face, and now she knew what the violent emotion inside her was. Fury. A soul-deep, burning, cleansing fury. He had almost destroyed her, had shattered her self-respect, humiliated and degraded and hurt her. He had forced her to run, to hide, to look over her shoulder in terror. He had turned her into a cowering animal.

No more. The sickening knowledge that he had watched them, leering in the shadows as his twisted presence intruded on an interlude of stark intimacy between her and Mitch, so enraged her that she could think of nothing else. He'd defiled so much of her, and she refused to let him cast his diseased shadow over the joy she had found with Mitch.

"You bastard," she said softly. "Sick, twisted—" She heard the rattle of savagery from his throat, but it had lost all power to frighten her. "If I wasn't sure you'd be roasting in hell someday, I'd burn you alive myself—"

Her unexpected defiance momentarily stunned Brad and, she realized later, gave Mitch the precious seconds he needed. As quick and silent as a cat, he crossed the upper terrace and vaulted over the balustrade, launching himself at Brad. The force of the impact sent the big silver gun spinning away and carried both men to the ground hard.

It happened so fast that Kelly couldn't move a muscle. In a crazily detached suspension, she saw them go down, the jarring collision knocking them apart so that they could both roll and scramble up. Mitch was first on his feet, still catlike in his swift, graceful precision; she had never thought of him as deadly, but that was in him now and visible, cold menace coming off him like arctic wind off a glacier. But Brad was enraged and almost as quick; he was inches taller than Mitch and forty pounds heavier, and there was an animal brutality in him that was totally alien to Mitch.

That brutish cunning was very much in evidence, because the first move Brad made was to try to blindside his enemy, to come at him on the left side. Only the fact that Mitch was still very conscious of his lost eye enabled him to anticipate the tactic and guard against it.

Her moment of detachment—actually very brief—allowed Kelly to see the first few moves of the battle as something almost as beautiful as it was deadly. Men had fought throughout their existence, and there was a curious primitive exhilaration in both these men that was almost palpable. Too many emotions had seethed in them both for too long; the physical struggle was something both wanted.

But Kelly's immobility lasted only a few seconds. She didn't doubt Mitch's ability to hold his own despite the seemingly unequal contest, but she had no intention of standing by idly while the battle raged. Brad had no comprehension of fair play, and she knew he'd pull something underhanded if he got the chance.

She looked around wildly for the gun, and realized immediately that it had been knocked into a riotous clump of ivy; she'd never be able to find it there. She hesitated for an instant, but the sickening thuds of flesh on flesh made her whirl for the steps leading up to the terrace and race into the house.

The gun was just where she'd put it, in the drawer of her nightstand. It was a .38, fully loaded and well kept; she'd taken lessons almost three years earlier in handling firearms, and had practiced her marksmanship at various pistol ranges. It had been a matter of necessity, something she had hated doing. But for the first time she felt no revulsion at the dull black gleam of the revolver and its heavy weight in her hand. Gripping the pistol firmly, she ran back downstairs and to the garden.

It seemed to her that an eternity had passed, but only minutes had gone by. Reaching the terrace, she ignored the steps, scrambled over the balustrade and into the lower garden, her eyes fixed on the two men. The marks of battle were showing on both men. Brad had a split lip and one eye looked swollen; he was also protecting his left side with his arm in a way that indicated either a bad bruise or a cracked or broken rib.

Mitch's mouth was also bleeding, and there was a reddening mark high on his right cheekbone that would be a bruise later.

No fan of any kind of fighting, Kelly had never before seen two adult men trying to kill each other with bare hands—and she never wanted to see it again. She couldn't help thinking that her very few glimpses of stylized boxing and wrestling were shockingly tame compared to the deadly speed and brute force of what she was seeing now.

They weren't going to stop. She realized that on some level of her mind. Even Mitch, whose initial motive had been to protect her, was now totally caught up in a primitive male struggle for supremacy. They were moving so quickly that she didn't dare risk a shot; eyes blind and chests heaving, utterly silent except for grunts of pain and effort, they were fighting to the death.

Brad must have realized he was going to lose. His greater height and weight should have given him the advantage, but it didn't. He had the bulky muscles that come from bench presses and chinups; Mitch had the raw strength of a body honed with painful effort to superb peak condition. The blows delivered by the more slender man had behind them the force of a pile driver, while his lightning-quick reflexes enabled him to deflect or completely avoid Brad's increasingly wild swings.

Brad couldn't stand losing. With the survival instinct of an animal, he took advantage of the uneven terrain of the garden, sacrificing pain for gain. He stopped trying to protect his cracked rib and charged toward the other man with furious swings. He felt the rib go completely under a well-placed blow, but Mitch had to give ground or be quite literally run over.

The low place was half hidden by vines of ivy, but Mitch wouldn't have seen it anyway. He stumbled and, his balance unable to compensate, went over backward.

Rather than press his advantage, Brad leapt back away from his fallen enemy and bent to claw at his ankle. An instant's grace, that's all he'd wanted. Just time enough. He straightened with a wicked knife in his hand. Mitch was already back on his feet, but he went still as a flat voice cut through the air.

"Brad."

For a heartbeat Mitch was surprised to see her there. The first hammerlike punch from the larger man had done something to him that he was only now aware of. His attack had been driven only by the need to protect Kelly, but when the first blow had staggered him, he had realized with a queer shock that this man had already hurt her. That he had used his great size and force against her delicate softness without mercy, teaching her a terror no woman should ever have to know. At that instant of realization a red haze had crept over his mind, and he had seen or heard nothing except the bastard he wanted to kill.

But she stood there now, her slight body still and her face pale, eyes that were now almost black fixed on West. She was closer to him, only a few feet away, and the gun in her steady two-handed grip was aimed at the center of his chest.

For an instant West looked almost ludicrously surprised. The knife in his hand was held with the expertise of a street fighter, loosely and in front of his body with the blade pointing up rather than down. He stared at his ex-wife as if he couldn't believe she would aim a gun at him.

"What the hell are you doing?" he barked, obviously having no idea how ridiculous the demand sounded.

"Drop the knife," she said flatly.

"You've never fired a gun in your life—"

She cocked the pistol. "The safety's off. There are no empty chambers. And I have a marksman's medal."

Bradford West stared at the scared rabbit he had hurt and taunted and pursued for years, and he must have seen what Mitch saw in her stony gaze. She wasn't afraid. She had defeated him simply by overcoming her fear of him. He must have seen that.

And he hated to lose.

With a roar of blind rage he lunged at her, the knife curving toward her slender body. Two shots cracked through the air, almost deafening and so close together they sounded like one. Brad staggered back, a look of surprise on his face as scarlet blossomed on his chest and shoulder, and fell heavily.

Kelly didn't see him fall. She looked back over her shoulder at the two men on the terrace. One was burly and casually dressed, while the other wore the reassuring uniform of a policeman; it was the cop's gun that had fired along with hers. She looked at her own gun and carefully thumbed on the safety, then dropped it to the ground and hurried to Mitch.

He met her halfway.

"Ouch."

Holding the antiseptic-soaked pad of gauze firmly to the corner of his mouth, she said, "You're going to have a lovely bruise on your cheek too. Are you sure the ribs are okay?"

"Just another lovely bruise, I promise you."

The house was quiet and they were alone—finally. The police and the coroner's wagon had departed, as well as the detective Mitch had hired. Evan Boyd had sincerely apologized to her for not having the sense to double-check his own assumptions.

He had assumed that Brad was safely in Texas because of references to his presence in a couple of newspaper articles. It had occurred to him only when he was killing time before boarding his flight that charity organizations generally gave the newspapers lists of those who had contributed to their functions—implying rather than stating actual presence.

Worried by that realization, he had called the investigator in Texas who had been helping him and suggested he go openly to Brad's office and find out for certain if he was there. In the meantime, Boyd decided that Brad would neither have brought a weapon registered to him from Texas, nor purchased one here in Oregon in his own name. So he called his policeman friend in Portland and they began checking the likely places.

Gun laws were strict, but to a man like Brad West, who was used to buying what he wanted, difficulties could be overcome. He had bought the big Magnum from a pawnshop the day before.

And once Boyd knew that a man matching Brad's description—right down to the charming smile—had bought a gun, he wasted no time in persuading his friend to accompany him back to the house. Increasingly worried, he had called Mitch from the car when they were still minutes from the house.

They'd made it just in time. Since a policeman had witnessed the fact that Bradford West had attempted to kill his ex-wife, no charges would be filed, even if an autopsy proved that it had been her bullet that had killed him.

Kelly didn't really care. She knew Mitch was concerned about her emotional state, but she hadn't had a chance to reassure him that she was fine. Taking the opportunity now, she said, "I won't have nightmares, you know."

"He didn't give you a choice," Mitch said quietly.

She wondered if that was why she felt nothing at all about Brad's death. "When I first started taking lessons at a pistol range, I thought I'd never be able to point that gun at a person. Even him. But today . . . well, I didn't feel hate or even a need for revenge. I just knew I wouldn't let him win."

Mitch tossed the gauze pad onto the coffee table and drew her into his arms. "He can never hurt you again."

"Or you. He meant to kill us both. I finally realized, while he was talking out there, that he literally couldn't live with the knowledge that another man had bested him. That's the way he saw it. No matter what he did, I . . . couldn't let go of you. It frustrated him that his—his rival was a ghost, but it was a hundred times worse when you were a flesh-and-blood reality. He watched us," she added softly. "In the conservatory."

His arms tightening around her, Mitch said, "I know. I heard part of what he said to you out there."

"It made me sick, that he'd done that. He made

so many things dirty, even words. I couldn't bear it that he'd tried to make us dirty too."

Mitch released her and rose from the couch, then took her hand and drew her up as well. He led her from the room. When she realized where he was taking her, her hand trembled in his.

"Mitch—"

He took her into the conservatory and eased her gently down on the chaise. "We're alone, sweetheart, I promise you. Nobody's watching us. There's no threat."

The late afternoon sunlight was shining through the glass all around them, making the plants glow emerald. The French doors were standing open so that a cool, moist breeze rustled through the leaves, and the ocean was a distant whisper.

"Mitch, I don't know if I can—"

"Shhh." He kissed her, apparently untroubled by any pain in his swollen, cut lip. He kissed her slowly and deeply, teasing her mouth until she relaxed and began to respond. Guiding her to lie back on the cushions, he slipped one hand underneath her blouse and stroked her side, still kissing her.

Kelly lost all awareness of everything except him and the heat rising inside her. She murmured a protest when his mouth left hers, then eagerly helped him get rid of her blouse and the camisole. She didn't know which of them had removed his shirt, but his smooth, hard skin was under her seeking hands, and she could feel his muscles moving with the sinuous power she loved. His mouth was on her breasts, and the heavy jeans slid free of her with the wisp of panties, and there was another muffled noise that might have been his pants being cast aside. Waves of pleasure rippled through her, each hotter than the last, and throaty sounds welled up and escaped her.

She felt his mouth moving lower, making her stomach quiver in tiny surges of electric delight. He was murmuring soft, rough things against her flesh, blunt sex words and tender love words, and the combination was so starkly intimate that it made her excitement spiral out of control. Then his heated caresses moved lower still, and she cried out when he found the aching fullness of her. Her body was out of her control again, and she was helpless to do anything except endure the burning wash of feelings. She was submerged in them, then lifting, trembling like a wild thing on the crest of a final huge wave. . . .

He rose above her and she cradled him frantically, her need pulsing through her with a primitive demand. She felt the slow, hot push inside her, and moaned as her body accepted him like a part of itself. He kissed her as his weight settled fully on her, roughly now and with fierce hunger, tangling his fingers in her hair, and she was kissing him with the same uncontrolled desire as she writhed beneath him.

Mitch had totally forgotten that the initial point of this had been to remove the taint of West's voyeuristic observance of their earlier lovemaking. As always, his desire for her had swamped every rational thought, carrying him along on a tide so devastating he half expected it to kill him. Her body clasped his with soft heat and slick tightness in a caress he would have happily died for, and she was moving with him, taking him so completely that they seemed a single being, striving together in a blinding white silence until the light splintered and the silence was filled with raw sounds of stark ecstasy.

His first coherent thought was that the damned chaise was so narrow he couldn't lie beside her and he didn't think he could bear to leave her completely. Forcing his drained muscles to support him, he eased himself up on his elbows and looked down at her. Her lovely face was rosy, and a sleepy half smile was on her lips. He kissed her tenderly, and soft purple eyes opened to gaze seriously into his.

"I've wanted to say it for days now, but I couldn't —until it was finished with him. That chapter *did* have to be ended. I had to stop running." Her voice was grave.

"I know."

Her smile changed, became so tender it almost stopped his heart. "I didn't think I'd ever be whole again. Then I opened the door and saw you there . . . and I began to realize that something inside me *had* waited for you. I love you, Mitch. I think I've loved you all my life."

He felt his throat close up even as some deeper part of him went suddenly still. So long . . . He'd waited so long to hear the words. And it was like being freed from a prison, watching the gate open and seeing before him a wonderful freedom. For the first time, he truly understood what love meant.

Holding a hand, not chaining a soul.

"I love you too, baby. God, I love you so much."

"Forever?" she whispered.

Whatever fate had in store for them, he knew nothing would alter that. "Forever."

• • •

She insisted that he soak in a hot bath that night, pointing out that his day had been more than usually active, then displayed an unexpected talent by giving him a massage that left him in a condition best described as boneless. He found the strength to hold her when she climbed into bed beside him.

And for the first time in more than a year, he slept through the night without stirring.

Nine

"Mitch?" Kelly returned to the den after answering the front-door bell, a slight frown between her brows. She was carrying a large manila envelope from which she'd extracted a sheaf of papers, and a smaller, legal-sized envelope.

"What's up?" He rose from rebuilding the fire and joined her as she sat down on the couch.

Nearly a week had passed since the shooting, and they'd made several trips into Portland for explanations and depositions and the like. The newspapers had finally relegated to back pages their follow-ups to the story. The police and district attorney had closed the case. This was the first peaceful day Kelly and Mitch had had together since then, and their morning had been interrupted by a Federal Express delivery.

"It's from my attorney in Baltimore," she murmured, still frowning as she read the cover letter. "He sent all the realtor's paperwork on the house. He isn't happy that he had to find out I was living here in the house from the realtor."

"Why should that worry him?" Mitch asked curiously.

"That's what I'm trying to— Oh. Oh, I see. He's been holding a letter that he was supposed to send to me as soon as I was in residence here. It was given to him the same time as—" Her eyes widened as she finished reading her lawyer's letter. Setting that and the other papers aside, she looked at the sealed legal-sized envelope that had been sent along, then lifted her gaze to Mitch.

"It's from your father."

"What?"

Kelly shrugged. "Maybe now we'll find out why he left me the house."

"I am curious about that," Mitch admitted, watching as she pried open the flap of the envelope. He saw her pull a slightly smaller envelope out, but didn't notice anything odd about it until she held it up for him to see.

On the front, written in a bold, rather heavy hand, were the names Kelly Russell and John Mitchell.

"Maybe you should open it," she murmured, handing him the envelope.

Mitch nodded and did so, more than a little puzzled. He recognized his father's handwriting, and automatically noted the date at the top of the first page of the letter; this had been written a month before Hugh Mitchell's death.

" 'Dear Kelly and John—' " Mitch broke off abruptly, adding almost to himself, "He's the only one who called me John."

Kelly half turned to watch his face, hoping with everything inside her that this letter wouldn't be something that would hurt Mitch. "If you want to read it to yourself," she began, but he shook his head with a quick smile.

"It's addressed to both of us."

She nodded and waited silently.

Mitch cleared his throat and continued reading aloud. " 'I don't ask your forgiveness; I'm told some things are meant to be, and that if my actions had been different, the end would still be the same. Perhaps I need to believe that, whether or not it's true. But I do want to tell you both I'm sorry my attitude made it harder for you.

" 'By now, John, I'm sure you've come to understand what a complex emotion love is. I wish I had understood sooner. I hope you learned something from my mistakes, and choose not to repeat them. Saying that you love is easy, but living up to those simple words is the most difficult thing you'll ever do. And the finest. I failed in that, but I believe you won't. Just remember that to love and be loved is the most important thing in life.' "

Mitch drew a deep breath. " 'Kelly, I'm sorry we never met. Whatever you may believe, I never hated you. I was afraid of losing John as I lost his mother, never realizing until too late that I had driven them both away with my possessiveness. I hope you can understand, and believe there was no malice in my objection to your marriage.

" 'As I write this letter, you, John, are still in a coma, and Kelly is struggling to go on with her life. The doctors tell me there's no hope my son will ever recover, and my attorneys are aghast at the instructions I have demanded they follow. I wonder myself if I have allowed false hope to ease the guilt and despair I've felt for so long. But I'm a hard-headed businessman, John, you know that, and hardly prone to believe in fantasies.

" 'Is this a fantasy, that you're reading my words? No. You are reading them. You and Kelly, together, in the house where you spent so many happy summers. It isn't summer there now, is it? Late winter, perhaps, or early spring. And the two of you have found each other again, despite fate.

" 'Or . . . because of fate. Some things are planned, I'm told, and I believe that. Some people are meant to be together, and I believe that as well. Perhaps I need faith of some kind at this very late stage of my life, but I think it is rather that I at last understand the power of love.

" 'Be kind to each other.' "

Mitch refolded the letter carefully, then looked at Kelly. "I—don't quite know what to make of that."

"Neither do I." She felt shaken on her own account, and was conscious of a deep compassion for Hugh Mitchell. "Did you notice that twice he used the phrase 'I'm told' as if . . ."

"As if someone were standing there explaining to him how you and I would be together," Mitch agreed slowly. "Maybe that's why he left you this house, so that I could find you."

"But how could he be so certain you'd come out of the coma? The doctors weren't giving him any hope, he said that. But he *knew*. He knew you'd be all right, that we'd be here. He arranged to have this sent as soon as I was living here, and I've been in the house only a couple of weeks; how did he know I wouldn't live here years ago, long before you came? And it is late winter, and we read his letter. . . ."

Mitch slipped an arm around her and held her close. "I don't know, sweetheart. But, as he said, he *wasn't* a man to believe in fantasy, I do know that; he wasn't an irrational or sentimental man. He would have believed the doctors—unless someone else convinced him they were wrong. Apparently, someone did."

"Who? A priest? What he said about some things being meant to be—"

"No, he wasn't religious. At least not that I remember. I don't know, Kelly. I just don't know."

She didn't know either. But she felt better now about Mitch's father, and she was glad he'd written the letter—whatever his beliefs had been. Mitch had been robbed of the chance to say good-bye to his father, to put things right between them, and the letter had helped ease that pain.

After all her protests that what they'd had together was in the past, and Mitch's insistence that the future was theirs, it was perhaps ironic that he now seemed content with the present. He told her often that he loved her, and she certainly had no doubts that he desired her physically; she felt so loved, in fact, that it occurred to her only gradually that Mitch was avoiding any mention of their future.

After thinking it over carefully, Kelly thought she understood the reason for his silence. And rather than let the situation go on, she chose to confront it obliquely.

"I'm not pregnant, you know."

It was late morning, and they'd gone out into the garden for a walk after breakfast. At her abrupt but conversational statement, Mitch stopped and stared at her. She wasn't at all surprised to see a flash of disappointment that was quickly veiled by lowered lashes.

"You aren't?" he said.

"No. I found out this morning. That was why I

was already fixing breakfast when you woke up. Cramps woke me, and since I had to get up anyway, I just stayed up. So, since we've been lucky this far, we'd better do something about birth control."

Mitch cleared his throat. "Do you want to take care of it, or should I?"

"I think I'd better. I have a feeling you'd forget." She stared up at him solemnly.

"Well, you do drive rational thoughts out of my head," he admitted.

"The first couple of days, maybe." Her tone was very gentle. "But after that, you were trying to get your own way."

"Kelly—"

"Of course, I should have realized sooner. And I should have brought up the subject before now."

"Why didn't you?" he asked, suddenly curious.

"Because I wanted a baby," she said baldly, and then, before he could say a word, added, "But I realized that I certainly didn't want to trap a man into marrying me, even if that *was* what he had in mind."

Mitch had the grace to look sheepish, but said, "I was trying not to push, dammit."

"And had your fingers crossed that I'd get pregnant?"

"Well . . ." He stared down at her with restless eyes.

She smiled suddenly. "Mitch, I do want a baby. But I think we deserve a little time alone together first, don't you?"

He sighed. "Yes."

"And," she said thoughtfully, "we should probably get married before we start a family."

Mitch went very still. Finally his voice emerged,

but it was flat with restraint. "I suppose I could move control of the company to the West Coast. Executive control, anyway. Leave the nuts and bolts back in Baltimore, at least for the time being."

She nodded. "That sounds feasible. And since I can work practically anywhere, I think here's a good place."

He cleared his throat, but his voice showed signs of strain when he said, "You haven't been wearing that ring, even on a chain. I was beginning to get worried."

Kelly slid her arms around his lean waist and gazed up at him seriously. "The man who gave me that ring never really asked me to wear it. That didn't matter then, but I think it does now. I think that *now* he wants a partner. Not a possession."

"A partner," Mitch agreed huskily as his arms lifted to encircle her. "And so much more. A lover. A friend. The little girl I read stories to and taught to hit a curve ball. The teenager who wobbled in high heels and put too much spray in her beautiful hair. The woman who's taught me so much about love, and about myself." He drew a deep breath. "I love you, Kelly. I love you so much. Will you marry me?"

"Yes." She lifted her face for his kiss, her violet eyes glowing with happiness. "I love you, Mitch. And I've been waiting all my life to marry you."

Epilogue

The old man with wise dark eyes in his benign face chuckled softly as he closed the file and laid it aside on his big desk. His elegant hands drew forward another unmarked folder, and he began studying the contents.

In the yellow glow of the lamp his white-bearded face was serious, but lurking in the depths of his discerning eyes was a gleam of undiminished delight.

"You're plotting," she said in the tone of one who knew him well.

"Naturally, my love." His voice was deep and rich, the glance he sent toward her chair a playful one.

"Should I pack?"

He studied the file a moment longer. "Yes. Yes, I believe you should."

THE EDITOR'S CORNER

May is a special month here at LOVESWEPT. It's our anniversary month! We began publishing LOVESWEPTs in May 1983, and with your encouragement and support we've been at it ever since. One of the hallmarks of the LOVESWEPT line has always been our focus on our authors. The six authors whose books you can look forward to next month represent what we feel is the true strength of our line—a blend of your favorite tried-and-true authors along with several talented newcomers. The books these wonderful writers have penned just for you are as unique and different as the ladies themselves.

Helen Mittermeyer leads off the month with the second book in her *Men of Ice* trilogy, **BLACK FROST**, LOVESWEPT #396. Helen's legions of fans often remark on the intensity of emotion between her characters and the heightened sense of drama in her novels. She won't disappoint you at all with **BLACK FROST!** Hero Bear Kenmore, a race-car driver with nerves of steel, gets the thrill of his life when he meets heroine Kip Noble. Bear has never met a woman whose courage and daring equals his own, but Kip is his match in every way. For Kip, falling in love with Bear is like jumping into an inferno. She's irrevocably drawn to him yet has to struggle to keep her independence. Helen has once again created characters who barely keep from spontaneously combusting when they're together. Helen's "men of ice" are anything but!

Jan Hudson's latest treat is **STEP INTO MY PARLOR**, LOVESWEPT #397. With three previous books to her credit, this sassy Texas lady has captured your attention and doesn't plan to let it go! She brings characters to life who are true to themselves in every way and as straightforward as Jan herself. You'll enjoy the ride as her unabashedly virile hero, Spider Webb, falls hard for lovely socialite Anne Foxworth Jennings. Anne is out of cash and nearly out of hope when she meets the seductive pirate, Spider. He almost makes her forget she has to stay one step ahead of the man who'd threatened her life. But in Spider's arms she's spellbound, left breathless with yearning. Caught in his tender web, Anne discovers that she no longer fears for her life because Spider has captured her soul. **STEP INTO MY PARLOR** will grab you from page one!

Joan Elliott Pickart's **WHISPERED WISHES**, LOVESWEPT

(continued)

#398, tells the love story of Amnity Ames and Tander Ellis. You may remember Tander as the sexy computer expert friend of the hero from **MIXED SIGNALS**, #386. Joan just had to give Tander his due, and he falls for Amnity like a rock! Can you imagine a gorgeous hunk walking into a crafts store and telling the saleswoman he's decided to take up needlepoint! Tander does just that and Amnity never suspects he's got ulterior motives—she's too busy trying to catch her breath. Joan's characters always testify to the fact that there is a magical thing called love at first sight. Her books help renew your spirit and gladden your heart. You won't be able to resist feeling an emotional tug when Amnity whispers her wishes to Tander. Enjoy this special story!

One of the newcomers to LOVESWEPT is Terry Lawrence—an author we think has an exciting future ahead of her. You may have read Terry's first LOVESWEPT, **WHERE THERE'S SMOKE, THERE'S FIRE,** which was published in the fall of 1988. Since then, Terry has been hard at work and next month her second book for us hits the shelves, **THE OUTSIDER,** LOVESWEPT #399. Both the hero and the heroine of this sensually charged romance know what it's like to be outsiders, and in each other's arms they discover what it feels like to belong. When Joe Bond catches Susannah Moran switching dice in the casino he manages in his Ottawa Indian community, he has to admit the lady is good—and temptingly beautiful. Just doing her job investigating the casino's practices, Susannah has to admit she's never been caught so fast and never by a man who set off alarms all over her body! These two special people don't find it easy to bridge the differences between their cultures. But what does come easily is the overwhelming need and desire they feel for each other. Terry will surely win loads of new readers with this tender, evocatively written love story. You'll want to count yourself among them!

We published Patt Bucheister's very first LOVESWEPT, **NIGHT AND DAY,** back in early 1986, and what a smash debut it was! Now, many books and many fans later, Patt presents you with another delicious delight, **THE ROGUE,** LOVESWEPT #400. A warm and generous lady with a sunny disposition, Patt naturally creates such a heroine in Meredith Claryon. When Meredith receives a strange phone call one night from a man demanding she answer his ques-

(continued)

tions, Meredith handles the situation with her usual grace and aplomb. Paul Rouchett is so intrigued by the lady he's never met that he decides he has no choice but to convince her to team up with him to find the embezzler who'd robbed his nightclub and run off with her sister. And what a team they make! The tart-tongued nurse and the owner of the Rogue's Den are an unbeatable duo—but discovering that. for themselves leads them on a merry, romantic chase. Patt's strong belief in love and romance couldn't come across better than in this well-crafted book.

Have you every wondered exactly what makes a guy a good ol' boy?. Having lived my entire life north of the Mason-Dixon line, I can tell you I have! But after reading **LOVIN' A GOOD OL' BOY** by Mary Kay McComas, LOVESWEPT #401, I wonder no more. Hero Buck LaSalle is a good ol' boy in the flesh, and when Yankee Anne Hunnicut hits town in her high heels and designer suits, Buck leaves no doubt in her mind about the term. He has the sexiest smile she's ever seen and too much charm for his own good, and although he's none too pleased about why she's there, he shows her in more ways than she ever imagined how much he wants her to stay. With her inimitable style, Mary Kay will have you giggling or sighing with pleasure or shedding a tear—probably all three—before you finish this sure-to-please romance. You'll long for a good ol' boy of your own.

Since we like to set the books in our anniversary month apart, we're going to surprise you with our cover design next month. But you're used to surprises from us, right? It makes life more interesting—and fun!

All best wishes.

Sincerely,

Susann Brailey

Susann Brailey
Editor
LOVESWEPT
Bantam Books
666 Fifth Avenue
New York, NY 10103

FAN OF THE MONTH

Jane Calleja

It was the colorful cover which prompted me to buy my first LOVESWEPT. I was already an avid reader of romance books then, but the unique stories and interesting characters in the LOVESWEPTs brought new meaning to romance for me.

New issues arrived here in the Philippines each month featuring original and delightful plots. I fell in love with the heroes and heroines of Barbara Boswell, Iris Johansen, Fayrene Preston, Joan Elliott Pickart, Kay Hooper, and Sandra Brown. The authors were able to capture everyday human emotions and make their characters come alive. I would like to thank these writers for answering my letters despite their hectic schedules.

My wish is to be able to join the ranks of the LOVESWEPT authors in the future. Right now I am nineteen years old and a third-year college student. I love reading LOVESWEPTs so much that I read the same books over and over again. In fact, I've read **FOR THE LOVE OF SAMI** by Fayrene Preston more than ten times, and I plan to read it again soon. Once I start to read, I really lose track of time and place. My family just watches me queerly if I suddenly giggle or cry in the middle of reading a book. That's how vivid LOVESWEPTs are! You can't help but feel what the characters are feeling.

I was surprised, but honored and delighted to be chosen a Fan of the Month. Thank you!

THE DELANEY DYNASTY

THE SHAMROCK TRINITY

☐ 21975 RAFE, THE MAVERICK
   by Kay Hooper $2.95

☐ 21976 YORK, THE RENEGADE
   by Iris Johansen $2.95

☐ 21977 BURKE, THE KINGPIN
   by Fayrene Preston $2.95

THE DELANEYS OF KILLAROO

☐ 21872 ADELAIDE, THE ENCHANTRESS
   by Kay Hooper $2.75

☐ 21873 MATILDA, THE ADVENTURESS
   by Iris Johansen $2.75

☐ 21874 SYDNEY, THE TEMPTRESS
   by Fayrene Preston $2.75

THE DELANEYS: *The Untamed Years*

☐ 21899 GOLDEN FLAMES *by Kay Hooper* $3.50

☐ 21898 WILD SILVER *by Iris Johansen* $3.50

☐ 21897 COPPER FIRE *by Fayrene Preston* $3.50

THE DELANEYS II

☐ 21978 SATIN ICE *by Iris Johansen* $3.50

☐ 21979 SILKEN THUNDER *by Fayrene Preston* $3.50

☐ 21980 VELVET LIGHTNING *by Kay Hooper* $3.50

- -

Bantam Books, Dept. SW7, 414 East Golf Road, Des Plaines, IL 60016

Please send me the items I have checked above. I am enclosing $_____
(please add $2.00 to cover postage and handling). Send check or money
order, no cash or C.O.D.s please.

Mr/Ms _____

Address _____

City/State _____ Zip_____

SW7—4/90

Please allow four to six weeks for delivery.
Prices and availability subject to change without notice.

60 Minutes to a Better, More Beautiful You!

Now it's easier than ever to awaken your sensuality, stay slim forever—even make yourself irresistible. With Bantam's bestselling subliminal audio tapes, you're only 60 minutes away from a better, more beautiful you!

__ 45004-2	**Slim Forever**	$8.95
__ 45112-X	**Awaken Your Sensuality**	$7.95
__ 45081-6	**You're Irresistible**	$7.95
__ 45035-2	**Stop Smoking Forever**	$8.95
__ 45130-8	**Develop Your Intuition**	$7.95
__ 45022-0	**Positively Change Your Life**	$8.95
__ 45154-5	**Get What You Want**	$7.95
__ 45041-7	**Stress Free Forever**	$7.95
__ 45106-5	**Get a Good Night's Sleep**	$7.95
__ 45094-8	**Improve Your Concentration**	$7.95
__ 45172-3	**Develop A Perfect Memory**	$8.95

NEW!

Handsome Book Covers Specially Designed To Fit Loveswept Books

Our new French Calf Vinyl book covers come in a set of three great colors— royal blue, scarlet red and kachina green.

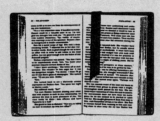

Each 7" × 9½" book cover has two deep vertical pockets, a handy sewn-in bookmark, and is soil and scratch resistant.

To order your set, use the form below.